Sins
&
Secrets

Sins & Secrets

Carolyn Chambers Sanders

WARNER BOOKS

NEW YORK   BOSTON

Copyright © 2005 by Carolyn Chambers Sanders
All rights reserved.

Warner Books

Time Warner Book Group
1271 Avenue of the Americas, New York, NY 10020
Visit our Web site at www.twbookmark.com.

Printed in the United States of America

ISBN 0-7394-5646-6

Book design and text composition by JAM design
Cover design by Christine van Bree
Cover photo by Pyre/Nonstock

I dedicate this book to my beautiful daughter and wonderful son, *Diondra Sanders* and *Dion Sanders, Jr.* Thank you both for being patient with mommy while I worked on this book, and thank you for giving me a reason and a purpose to complete this project.

I also dedicate this book to my sister *Brenda Banks* and my brother *Jerrold Chambers,* for supporting and believing in me. I love you all with all my heart.

CONTENTS

Contents

Sins
&
Secrets

ONE

I need you
I want you
Come do me right,
Please hold me and
make love to me . . .

if only for one night

I was so in love! He had everything I wanted and needed in a man at that time. He possessed all the qualities that captured and kept a woman's attention. He had the type of personality that made women want him, the sweetness, kindness, and gentleness that keeps a woman longing for more.

He had skills! Damn, that man has skills! Oh yeah, this beautiful chocolate-colored man loved me down oh so good that when he touched me, I melted like butter on a hot skillet. When his succulent, full lips were kissing me softly, I closed my eyes, took a deep breath and absorbed his sweetness.

He had all the good stuff that a woman needs. When he held me, I felt safe and warm, and I knew that was where I belonged—at least at that moment. This gorgeous specimen, who treated me like his precious queen when I needed it the most, was mine, but only for the night.

When I met . . . well, let's just call him Mike—I was at a small party with a few friends. I was bored and had been ready to leave for over an hour. Not wanting to be a hater, I stayed. As I sat and waited, I notice a rugged-looking but nevertheless fine man watching me. I turned my head and pretended not to see him because I was on a sabbatical from men. Two and a half years earlier, I ended my most emotionally draining long-term relationship. It was the kind of relationship where a woman gives everything she has and more, but is never appreciated. So getting involved was not on my agenda. I wasn't feeling a relationship, a lover, or even a one-night stand. At that time, I wanted no part of a man. No matter the cost, I tried to avoid the roller coaster of abuse and pain that comes with relationships.

I felt him watching, then he walked toward me. For some strange reason, my heart began to beat faster. A man I didn't know was having this kind of effect on me. He hadn't said anything to me or touched me, but I felt his presence. Since I had purposely avoided men for over two years, my reaction was not a good sign.

He stopped in front of me, but I looked away, ignoring his presence. Before I could decide what I wanted to say, he whispered, "Can I have you?"

I raised my head and looked into his eyes. I thought about how sweet his body smelled and how I felt his energy flowing through me. The chemistry was there, and girl, was I feeling every wave of his electricity. Looking very serious, I stared deep into his eyes and answered him by asking, "For how long and to do what with?" Even though I could've gotten naked right then and there, I knew I had to give him the obligatory hard time. Mama ain't raise no hoe.

He seemed confused by my response and asked me to repeat it. I confidently replied, "Did you or did you not ask me if you could have me?"

Looking even more perplexed, Mike responded, "Yeah."

I think he may have thought I was crazy or something, so I made clear to him that I knew exactly what I was doing.

"Well, I am asking you how long do you want me, and while you have me, what do you want to do with me? How I answer your question depends on how you answer mine." He, for some reason, found himself at a loss for words. So I continued, speaking very slowly and clearly: "Do you want me for a month, a week, or one night? Do you want to talk to me, hold me, make love to me, fuck me, or what? Exactly what do you want?"

He touched my hand and said, "I don't know how long I want you, but I want you now, tonight. Let me take you to a new level of pleasure, and give you the one thing I know no one else can give you, true ecstasy."

"Ecstasy!" I thought to myself. "I hope this fool don't think I'm taking some dope with him. I may have smoked a joint every now and then, but I ain't no dope fiend. Now, if he just talkin' about physical ecstasy then we can work something out, cause the nigga is so sexy."

I stood up, leaned in close and asked, "How are you supposed to do that?"

"Please don't let him say 'by taking this'," I prayed.

He gently lifted my chin and said in his deep, raspy voice, "Let me show you."

I stroked him lightly on the side of his face, licked his lips, and whispered, "Let's go."

I followed Mike to his car; I didn't have a second thought

about what I wanted this man to do. The image of our naked bodies intertwined excited me. At the same time, I tried not to imagine what the night would be like because I didn't want to be disappointed. You know how sometimes you expect so much, but get so little? I know ya feel me!

The road seemed to disappear into the darkness as we drove. His radio played one of those old school Prince songs that makes you feel all freaky. Damn, he smelled even better with the windows rolled up. It was a light cinnamon musk oil that must've been spread over his body. It all seemed like a late-night R&B music video, until the car slowed down in front of a hotel. For some reason my heart started beating fast like I was about to run a race or something. "Candice, get a grip on yourself, it's only a dick, not like you never had one before," I had to say to myself to calm down.

We checked in without speaking; our eyes said it all. Once we were in the room, I told him I wanted to take a quick shower, but he said that the smell of my body excited him. He wanted me just the way I was. I thought to myself, "I have to buy more of this body gel."

Then it all hit me. "What in the world am I doing?" Candice, you better than this. I can't do this. No . . . no, I can do this. Life ain't stopping because my panties ain't been dropping, but I have to do things on my terms.

Still possessing some doubt, I turned to him and said, "I haven't made love to a man in over two years, so I don't know why I want you, but I do. We don't know each other, but right now that doesn't matter because we're already here."

Before I could say another word, he put his sweet lips on mine, and we kissed passionately. He tasted delicious. I knew he had been drinking, but I didn't taste or smell the liquor. This excited me even more. He was naturally sweet.

As our mouths parted, I swept my tongue along my bottom lip. Hmmm . . . I could still taste beads of his sugary juices in my mouth.

I began to undress, but he stopped me.

"I don't want you to do anything; just enjoy what I'm about to do."

In a tone just above a whisper, he told me, "Lie down, I'll unwrap you in due time."

As I watched him take his clothes off, my body shivered all over. His body was sculptured like a chocolate-covered Hercules and did not have an ounce of fat on it. As I admired his beautiful body, I closed my eyes and knew that this was going to be good. His D was so pretty, not huge, but it was above average with a slight curve to it.

When I opened my eyes, he was looking at me. His dark, piercing eyes said that he wanted me, and he wanted me badly.

He lay down next to me and held me in his granite-chiseled arms. As he ran his hands through my hair, he whispered, "Relax," and lightly kissed my ears. While he was licking my ears, he said, "I know that this is going to be special, so I don't want to rush this. We have all night, so let's make the best of it."

I don't know why, but this moment felt like my first time. Only this time around, I wasn't cramped in the backseat of a car. And I definitely knew how to drive a stick now.

While he unbuttoned my shirt, he promised not to disappoint me. Tenderly, he said, "If there is something you need or want tonight, and I don't do it exactly the way you want me to, tell me. Tonight is your night, and I want to give you everything you have been missing and more."

Yeah, yeah, I know. The man is what most women dream about, he is fine, sexy as hell, and unselfish behind closed doors. What more can a woman ask for?

He kissed me again and told me to turn over. As I lay on my stomach, he simultaneously massaged my back and legs, and gave me little wet kisses and lustful licks all up and down my spine. I was feeling so good that my body began to move slowly. All I could do was tremble uncontrollably.

He moved me over on my back and gently kissed my breasts. He licked and kissed my breasts so softly that I found myself saying, "Oh I want you, I want you now."

In a low, barely audible rumble, he replied, "No, not yet; I haven't finished loving your body."

Then, he massaged my feet and kissed my toes. As he rubbed, licked, and kissed every part of my feet and legs, he caressed my inner thigh. I couldn't do anything but tell him how good he was making me feel.

"Ewww baby, don't stop. That feels so good."

The slight touch of the tip of his tongue on my clit sent me out of control. I moaned loudly, hoping that the sinful pleasures would never end. After he rubbed me, licked me, and caressed me from head to toe, front to back, and did not miss a spot, he whispered in my ear, "Do you want it now?"

I whimpered, "Yes, please, give it to me, give it to me now. But first put your condom on." Like I said before, Mama ain't raise no hoe, or should I say, Mama ain't raise no fool.

He obliged.

"Now it's time."

When he entered me, I screamed, not from pain, but in total ecstasy. I didn't remember it being this good, and I knew that no one had ever made love to me like this before. He was so gentle with me.

He kissed me, passionately, as he moved so perfectly inside me. We changed positions while he stayed inside me. Each position felt better than the one before. We carried on for most of the night, and it was feeling so damn good. So damn good!

I finally begged him to stop, and I cried as I told him that I couldn't take any more. I cried because I couldn't do anything else. After all of the moaning, screaming, and yelling, all that was left were my tears. Sex had never been so good that it made me cry. When I cried, he came.

He asked me if he gave me everything I needed and wanted. I told him he gave me everything and more, and he gave me what he promised, ecstasy.

He held me close to him for the rest of the night, and I melted in his arms. It all felt so perfect. When we woke up later Saturday morning, we showered together and started all over. I don't know how long we made love, but afterward, we held each other again.

Being in his arms was like being in a warm blanket on a cold winter morning. I was a woman again. Actually, I was a woman for the first time.

We called room service for brunch and slept for most of the day. When we woke up, we got dressed, hugged, and said our good-byes. As he asked me for my phone number, I put my finger on his lips so he couldn't finish. I said, "Let's just leave it here. I really enjoyed you and I thank you for what you gave me, but I am not ready for anything more." I continued to look into his eyes and said, "I really felt like I loved you last night."

This all seemed like a scene from one of those new black movies. You know, the ones with beautiful people doing things you thought you could never do, but always wanted to.

I gave him a long passionate kiss, said thank you, and walked off. It took everything in my body not to look back; I knew that if I had, I would have never left.

The drive home was pleasant. I smiled as I thought about the night. For Mike, it was probably just a screw. For me, it was the beginning of the rest of my life. The hurt and pain of my last relationship won't stop me from loving again, but now I'm doing it by my rules. I had forgotten how good it feels to give myself to a man. It was a beautiful experience, but I knew that it was only for one night, and no more.

As I continued to think about the night, the phone rang. It was Toi. "Girl, where have you been? I've been trying to reach you all night."

I told her that I had met this man, gone to bed with him, and that it was the best lovin' I'd ever had.

Shouting in my ear, she screamed in excitement, "Stop lying girl, stop lying! No you didn't let some nigga tear down the cobwebs! I don't believe you. Meet me for breakfast in the morning. I want to hear every little nasty detail."

TWO

A good woman is supportive of
her man in every way,
But he doesn't appreciate her
no matter what she does or say,
He disrespects her and always
seems to tear her down,
And when she really needs him
he can not be found,
Let him go, you don't need him
You are a precious pearl,
Ladies, remember . . .

it's a woman's world

We decided to meet at Grandma's Restaurant, which is located in the hood across the street from a park. While I was waiting for Toi and Amber to arrive, two guys sitting in the booth in front of me began flirting. They were winking, sticking their tongues out, and rubbing on their Johnsons; acting like pure fools. There is just no hope for some niggas. I actually felt sorry for these two because they really didn't have a clue.

Who I really felt sorry for were the women that liked this

type of stupidness. I realized a long time ago that men only do things that somebody responds to. And with all the dumb women around here, I'm sure that some of their stupid antics have pulled in many a number, and probably gotten them some booty too.

I ignored their sexually harassing advances; not only were they ignorant, but both of them were tore up from the floor up.

I know he is not coming over to talk to me, oh no, don't come over . . . stop, stop . . . "Hi, what's your name?" I really wanted to ignore him, but I didn't. It's not like me to break a brotha's self-esteem down, so I sat as he talked about nothing.

"Blah, blah, blah . . . you so fine. Blah, blah, and smart too," he uttered.

When I finally decided to look up at him, the only thing I could see was that booger hanging from his nose. I didn't look at him again because the big crusty green hunk of mucus made me sick. Every other word he said he sniffed snot back, "ssnnaa," up his nose, like a small child would do.

Girl, what do men be thinking about? They should at least make sure their nose is clean and their breath ain't stinkin' before they come in ya face. And a nigga wonder why a female act like she don't want to be bothered. Half of the time the nigga that approach you ain't worth yo time anyway, but you take a chance, because you are lonely, knowing that it ain't gonna amount to nothin'. Months later, you mad at yourself thinking, "Damn, that's one dick I could've done without."

Finally, I got tired of looking at that nasty green booger

stuck to his nose, so I touched my nose, trying to give him a sign—but no, it didn't work.

I couldn't take it any longer, "You have a booger hanging from your nose."

He kept talking for a few more seconds before he stopped.

"Who me?"

"No you."

Girl, can you believe this nasty Negro wiped the booger with his hand. Now that really bothered me. What happened to good old home training? I don't know this man's mama, but she needs to beat his raggedy behind.

I said, "You should probably go wash your hands before you eat." I was actually thinking, "Before you try to shake my hand or touch me."

He got up with a "why you worried, bitch" look on his face and walked toward the bathroom still twirling the booger around on his finger tips.

I watched him because I knew what was coming next . . . I'd be god damn; no he didn't. This fool put the booger in his mouth! He ate the damn thang. Nasty nigga, just a nasty, nasty nigga! My stomach turned watching this mess. To take my mind off his nastiness, I had to think about something else, something more pleasant.

I looked out the window and realized how beautiful the day was. The sun was shining, and it wasn't even noon yet. Lakes Park was full of people. This is not surprising; every time I eat at Grandma's, there is always something going on in the neighborhood.

Kids played ball in the streets, teenagers snuck kisses and

the old men argued over dominoes. But I have also seen dozens of fights, and late at night, people getting booty in their cars and in the park.

You grow up fast in the hood. Everything happens around you. Whether you want it to be a part of your surroundings or not, it becomes a part of you.

Life is just one big cycle. The same things go on at Lakes Park now that were going on back in the day, when I was a child. The only change is that the park is more run-down, but since they put a police station right next to it the dealers are selling less dope out of it.

Walking to school in fifth grade, I saw drug dealers on the street corners waiting for the next crack addict to come and spend their kid's welfare checks. During school hours, the rich folks' kids that lived in Palm Beach would drive across the bridge to buy drugs. When the hustlers saw the Bentleys, Mercedes, or limousines coming over the bridge, they would literally kill to make the sell. They knew that at least a thousand dollars would be spent in one transaction. With N.W.A., Kool G Rap, and Ice-T banging out of everybody's radio, the whole vibe was like *New Jack City* or something.

By the time I was in high school, I was friends with most of the hustlers on the streets. They watched out for me. I never had any girlfriends back home. They all hated me, because I excelled at everything I did and accomplished every goal I had set for myself. They expected me to fail since my mother was on crack, but I used her problems to strengthen and encourage me. Watching my mom fall apart helped me to know at an early age what I didn't want in my life. Compared to the kids in my hood, I stood out like a basketball player in Japan. I was taller than most girls, red-skinned, and had a head full of curly locks. I made all A's in school and was captain of the track team. I wasn't afraid to take or give a butt whipping. I looked like a pushover, but everyone knew that I would fight if I had to and win by any means necessary.

The older I became, the more the hustlers tried to make me one of their "girls." It's funny; I never fell into the trap. I didn't give up the coochie easy, but I did get money from them. I made them think that if they were good to me, then maybe they would get to paradise. I had what they wanted, a tight virgin twat. And they definitely had what I wanted—money.

Don't get me wrong, my life at home wasn't exactly horrible. I had the mere basics needed to survive. I ate one meal a day instead of three. I wore store brand clothes and shoes, instead of name brand. That was more than my mom could afford when she was living and before she got on crack, but I wanted more. I wanted what the superstars seemed to have, everything. No, "I wanted it all." And then some.

Hanging out with hustlers made me realize that there had to be a better way out. I wanted more for my mom and me. I knew that one day I would have all that I wanted. It upset me that my mom died before she could enjoy my success with me.

Ambition is a mother. If you desire something enough, there isn't nothing that can stop you from getting it.

I would drive across the bridge to Palm Beach and cruise Ocean Boulevard just to look at the huge mansions on the coast. Everyone had a mansion over there—John F. Kennedy's family, the Kellogg's cereal owner, Donald Trump, and a lot more people I can't think of right now. The huge iron gates that opened on demand, with the long driveways lined with hundreds of pine trees leading up to the main house, excited me.

I wanted to live like the people in Palm Beach and I wasn't going to let anything or anyone stop me.

I had to make a plan that ensured my success. No matter what it took, I was going to have it all.

During my college years, I didn't give it up for free and love wasn't in my vocabulary. I learned how to play the street game at an early age. I knew how to get the money I needed without compromising my self-respect. I drove a new Camaro at Florida A&M University and owned a three-bedroom house by the end of my first year.

Not bad for an average girl from the hood, huh?

I rented two of the rooms out, one to Amber and the other to Toi. We have been best friends ever since those days, though I have different friendships with each of them.

I remember Amber talking to someone on the phone one night; she didn't know I was listening. I never had girls around me that weren't jealous of me, so her description was surprising. She said, "She's beautiful, sexy and classy." The person she was talking to must have asked her to describe me in more detail, because she continued, "Well, she's tall and statuesque, has a body like a model with curves, nice full breasts, exotic striking features with big brown eyes that tantalize those who come in contact with her. She knows what she wants and is not afraid to go and get it. She always has a master plan and backup plans. The word 'can't' is not a part of her vocabulary. She is very confident, but not cocky. She doesn't try to prove herself because she says that she knows who she is. She's outgoing and some might consider her aggressive. She loves a good challenge. She is kindhearted and sweet, but no punk."

Damn, I thought I was the only one who knew I was that tight. I'm just joking, but I was flattered by her compliments.

As I listened to Amber, I knew that we would be friends. Most women can't say anything positive about another woman, but she made me sound almost perfect.

My hard work was finally paying off. People were beginning to see me as a success already.

I worked hard in college. I knew that my books came first and fun later. I schemed money from hustlers to buy my house and pay my bills. I made each one of them feel special, like they were the one who had my heart. I was adamant about finishing college. I did not hesitate to let them know that if they could not contribute, then, "Hey, see ya." I tried to work when I first got to school, but after three months of working ten hours a day and going to school full-time just to bring home a check worth only eight hundred dollars after taxes, I knew I had to do something different. I could hustle up in a few days the money I had made in a month. So I quit my job.

Oh no, don't get me wrong, I didn't sell myself. I got inside their heads, then I took control of their minds. I just made a nigga think that if he was good to me, then he just might get to candy land. However, only a select few were granted access to my private paradise.

Sitting alone in this room filled with so many different voices allowed me to reminisce more about how beautiful and therapeutic last night had been. I needed that. I needed everything Mike had given me. He relaxed me and pampered me. He was very sensual, and he gave me all of him, every seemingly perfect part. I can't think of anything that would have made last night better than it was. Tell me, what's better than a nigga who screws you good? One who can hold an intelligent conversation, loves your entire body, eats you like a bowl of melting ice cream, then makes love to you with a hard stiff cock like there's no tomorrow. Damn, it was good!

As I allowed my mind to wander off, Amber and Toi finally showed up. "What's up, girlfriend? All a diva wanna know before we even start our conversation is . . . was the dick good?" Toi being her loud usual self came in asking questions before she could even sit down good.

One thing that trips me out about Toi is that she can be so ghetto at times. But if you catch her during business hours, she transforms to Ms. Corporate America.

Toi is an entrepreneur, self-made, and will not let anything or anyone stop her. Money drives her; the more she make the more she wants. She lives to make the next dollar and does. She doesn't hesitate to use all the resources at her disposal to get what she wants. She will even sacrifice her body. She often said that if most women had a dollar for every man they screwed, most of them would be millionaires. She has an awesome physique, five-eight, has an athletic build, nice-sized breasts, bowed legs, and a very sexy walk. She is pecan tan and has attitude out of this world.

Most women think they are God's gift to men, but don't admit it. Toi thinks she's God's gift to men and women and has no trouble letting you know this. Let's just say she has a lot of confidence.

"I don't believe she gave up the cat. Now if you said that she let a nigga eat the coot, I'd believe that. You know that if a sista ain't getting the D, she still needs a good licking every now and then."

"Candice likes her cat ate, but she ain't screwing a thang. That's what happens to those liberated 'I don't need a man in my life' females who masturbate all the time. They forget how good the D really feels," Amber added.

Amber's comment made me pause.

In the back of my mind, I couldn't help but wonder, 'What the hell had I done?' I just screwed a man that I didn't even know; was I really being a hoe? Nah, I just got what I wanted at that time. Anyway I'm long overdue for taking control of me and some good lovin' from a tall dark and beautiful handsome stranger was what I needed to release all the pressure.

The repercussions may be good or cause pain, but I've learned that sometimes in life you do things that don't necessarily make sense, but they make you feel good. Sometimes you have to hurt in order to really learn how to appreciate life's pleasures.

After quietly thinking for a moment, I replied, "Girls, I can't give this good stuff to just anybody, nigga gotta earn it. Men don't want to do what it takes to get a taste of the 'almighty.'"

Regardless of my doubts, I refuse to let anyone know. It

seems like when a person comes into your inner space . . . that inner you, that only you know, you get hurt.

Amber asked, "Well, what did the nigga do last night to get it?"

I don't give a damn about that, what a female really wanna know is why you sexed a nigga you don't even know when you have hundreds of them that will do anything to get with you.

"That nigga must have some strong game or something. Was it the game or was it the big chocolate pole that he stuck deep down in yo hole," Toi amusingly said as she and Amber gave each other a high-five.

As I told them all the juicy details about my night, they both sat in silent awe. Ladies, you know we want to hear every little detail, so I had to make sure I didn't leave anything out. When I finished, Toi said, "Damn, that nigga laid that pipe down on you. Girl, it ain't many out there that knows how to work what they got and give it to you just like you want it. Damn, I know it was real good."

Amber said, "Damn, I need a man to take care of me like that! The last two I've had were a waste of time. Honey, one nigga did not know how to work what he had and he did not last five minutes."

Toi interrupted and said, "Two minutes . . . two minutes and counting," meaning that he came as soon as he put it in.

Women, y'all already know that those "I'm a Mandingo slinging D" niggas usually are knocked out before round one gets going good. Most of us wish we could find a minute, at least we could have a decent chance of getting some satisfaction out of being a throw pillow with a wet hole for some grunting and groaning fool.

Amber continued, "And the other couldn't lick the kitty to save his life."

"I can testify to that," I said. I was walking past her room door at her house when all I heard was "smaa, smaaa." It sounded like a dog licking and smacking at the same time. Me being the pervert I am, I had to peek in. Amber was lying on the bed, spread-eagled, looking disgusted, as if she wanted to ask the dude with his mouth between her thighs, "What are you doing?" His head was moving up and down, and he was making a loud smacking noise. I stood there laughing quietly because from the look on her face he hadn't licked the right spot yet. I wanted to tell him, "Open it up and lick the clit, more tongue action, less head moving." But, instead I just walked out.

Amber then commented, "I wish you would have. The only reason I went to bed with him anyway is because he bragged about how good he can eat the cat, and girl, was he a BIG disappointment. His tongue felt like a wet piece of sandpaper."

Out the blue, Toi asked me, "Did you cum?"

"Yeah I did, more than once."

"No, I don't mean while he was eating the kitty, but while he was inside of you?"

I swear to you, when she said that I could feel him inside me. I damn near nutted trying to answer her.

"That nigga's like the bomb uuh, did I!"

"Stop lying, girl, stop it, you never come like that! Damn, I would've paid anythang to see that there! So the nigga broke you down. He laid that pipe down, huh girl? It must've been one of those good hard ones? Damn, how many years has it been since you bust a nut like that?"

Then it dawned upon me: I had never experienced an orgasm like that before. I thought people were just playing when they say as you get older, you can control your body better. I guess I had control . . . control of me.

"Girl, I can't remember, but that thang was good, and we were somehow emotionally connected. I ain't gon' lie, I can't explain it."

"Did you suck his D? "

Don't front, you know you do it too. How can you expect to be done up proper if you don't return the favor? I think everybody gotta little freak in them.

"No, but I wanted to because his sweat was so sweet. I licked him dry and, girl, did he taste good."

"Well, did you get the digits?"

"No."

"Why not girl, that's the kind of man you keep on call because you know he can deliver with a guarantee."

"That's the problem, it was too good and something that good can be dangerous. I'm not ready for the challenge. I wasn't looking for a man or lover, I just needed to be made love to."

"No girl, you just needed some good, nasty lovin'."

I didn't say it out loud, but I knew that she was right.

"And you better believe that I did get what I wanted and needed."

Our waiter came over and asked us if we had decided on our order. "Yes, we'll have two nuts," Toi said jokingly.

Looking confused, the young unshaven waiter said, "Nuts? What kind do you . . ."

"No, girl. We need sweat to go with that. . . . We'll have two nuts on sweat," I said. We all started laughing.

Amber said, "It's something about the smell of a clean man's sweaty balls that turn me on. Make me want to just get on him and start riding . . . heee haw." Amber started turning her hand in the air like she was roping a horse.

The waiter looked at us like we were crazy and said, "Tell me when y'all wanna order food." Then he walked off.

"Girls, look who's walking in. Look at that hoe Shaniqua," Toi said.

Shaniqua hated us. There's nothing worse than having a sour whore in your business. She just made up stuff about us to talk about, and she can't stand Amber. She knows Amber is screwing her man, Randy. But Randy is screwing everybody, he's everybody's man.

I'll tell you more about this sorry nigga a bit later.

When Shaniqua saw us, she really put on the fake walk. When she twisted past our table, she started throwing her hips from side to side and swinging that weave like it was her hair.

Well, she paid for it so it was hers for a while.

When she walked past, Amber said very loudly, "Hate it, wouldn't want to be it." We all started to laugh very loudly.

She turned around, rolled her eyes, and said, "Stupid hoes."

Amber replied, "You the stupid hoe because that sweetness you taste on ya man's tongue is my honey sweet juices!"

Shaniqua got so upset that she couldn't order. She said, "Dykes," and walked out the restaurant. We blew her kisses as she sped off in her car.

Although I know that Shaniqua hated on us every chance she could with whoever would listen, I knew how she felt.

Always trying to get ahead but never can because she don't have enough willpower to keep going when thing get stuff. She just gives up and accepts the defeat. With that attitude and low self-esteem she will never get ahead; that is why I felt kinda bad for her and what we had done. Oh well, that's life. Maybe she had done something in a former life that made her deserve this treatment, or maybe she should stop doing what she's doin'. Always in bed wit somebody's man.

Toi said in a half giggle, "Look at ya divas, that's why them hoes don't like ya now." Me, Toi, and Amber were as thick as glue. We did almost everything together. When women see us out together they get jealous. I never understood why people hated on us so much because, believe me, we worked hard for what we have. No one gave us a damn thing. We grew up in the ghetto, went to college together, and did what we had to do to start our own businesses. We understood that business came first; then, and only then, can we afford to have fun. All it takes is a dream, ambition, and dedication to achieve what most might feel is unattainable.

A lot of folks fall victim to that Cinderella complex crap. You know—a great prince will come someday to give you everything you ever wanted. In reality, the only thing that's free is problems. You have to make opportunities, not wait on them. Ladies, keep that in mind.

I especially worked damn hard because I never wanted to depend on a man. I don't need no man telling me when to come, when to go, what to say and not say. I don't need a nigga who goes out all week, and only comes home when he wants to screw. But when a man is taking care of you, he feels like he can do that. And, you know what? He can, because he's calling the shots. You're a piece of furniture . . . he uses you when he gets ready . . . and when he's not, you are expected to be quiet, and wait until he wants to use you again. Who needs that bull?

As I was saying before, we go through a lot in the business world. Just dealing with the dirty old men in corporate America who want some fresh young cat is enough in itself.

Women have to earn respect, no, demand it, in the corporate realm because it's not given freely. This is definitely a fact when you are black, successful, know what you want out of life, and are willing to do what it takes to get it.

Yeah, women hated us because we had money and enjoyed life. But like Toi always said, "I don't know why those hoes are jealous. They don't know how many dicks I had to suck to drive this Rover. Shit, put them hoes in my shoes, and they won't last a day."

Toi worked long hours. She was dedicated to her success and making her money. She would stay up for days if she had to meet a deadline. However, she did not have a problem using her womanhood for favors.

One of my many mottoes is to enjoy life while we are young. When you grow older, no one remembers what you did anyway. As long as you are not hurting anyone intentionally, and you can live with what you do, then fuck 'em, fuck 'em all!

We finally left Grandma's and made plans to meet up later. We were going to a corporate function, and out to a club. Sundays were the best night to party. Everybody who was somebody came out, so the three divas definitely had to be in the house. I had had a long weekend and needed to relax before we went out, so I went home to shower and rest for a few hours.

As I was getting out of the shower my phone rang.

"I need you to come over. I need you to come over now!"

Amber was trying to talk while she was crying, but I couldn't understand all she was saying.

"What's wrong?"

"Just come over now!" Amber said, and then the phone went dead.

I threw on some jeans and hopped in my car. I almost hit some idiot in a Toyota as I flew through the street. I tried over and over to call her from my cell.

"Damn, still no answer."

I didn't know what to think, feel, or whatever. All I knew was that my friend needed me.

"Toi! Call an ambulance, I think something's really wrong with Amber. I can't talk now, but get over to her house right now! I'm almost there."

I came to a screeching halt in her driveway and ran to her house without cutting my car off.

"Amber!! Amber!!"

When I burst through Amber's door, I couldn't believe what I saw. She was lying helpless on the floor. Her face had been badly beaten and her eyes were swollen shut. The chair was broken in her room, and a handful of her hair had been pulled out and was lying next to her. She wasn't moving. Was she alive?

THREE

When I was down, you were there for me,
Your love and friendship have been the key,
You held me together when I couldn't take any more,
Now I understand . . .

what friends are for

I felt Amber's pulse to see if she was alive. She was. As I looked at her bruised face and body, I felt her pain. I sat next to her, gently put her head in my lap, and softly spoke to her. Not knowing if she heard me, tears rolling down my face, I rubbed my fingers lightly through her hair trying to comfort her. I just wanted to let her know that she wasn't alone.

Amber had always been there for me. Why?! Dammit, why was this happening?

She opened her eyes for a split second and tried to say something, but nothing came out. "I'm here, honey. I'm here, don't worry; I'm gonna take care of you."

She tried to smile to assure me that she was OK, but she was too weak to smile. I can't explain the hatred that swelled in my heart at that moment. Anger took over every emotion I had. I knew Randy had done this, and I wanted him to pay. This was not the first time he had done this to her.

As I continued to look at Amber, I felt sorry for her and could feel her pain, but I became furious with her. Randy had hit her before and had given her a black eye. She allowed him to treat her this way. She shouldn't have gotten involved with the no-good idiot anyway. Everyone has the right to decide what they want in life, regardless of who agrees or disagrees, but this was a bad decision.

Look at me, trying to be judgmental at a time like this. Right now all of that doesn't matter, but making sure that Amber is going to be all right does. Truth be told, I was just getting a grip on my own personal life. But this, this would prove to be a wake-up call. A wake-up call for all of us.

And, although life consists of taking chances, sometimes we have to sit back and analyze the situation. Then, we can decide if the consequences are really worth our choices and/or sacrifices. In this case, Randy wasn't bringing anything to the table but a bunch of bull. He was jealous, despite the fact that Amber wasn't his woman. They were friends, or should I say screwin' partners. He was screwin' every trick in town, but still tried to regulate the cat.

Randy is one of those sorry, good-for-nothin' niggas. He didn't deserve my friend. I know his itty-bitty weiner can't be worth a face of bumps and lumps.

Toi had already called the ambulance, but she arrived first. She walked in all hysterical, crying and screaming, so I had to calm her down. I told her that it wasn't doing Amber any good to hear her upset. I asked her to call to see how far the ambulance was from the house.

I couldn't move. I sat there frozen with my friend's blood all over my pants and shirt. What was happening? Maybe this was all some dream. Maybe . . .

The paramedics finally arrived with their sirens blaring loudly.

"What happened here ma'am?"

"I don't know!" I said.

"Is she conscious? Does she have any allergies?"

"We don't know, just help her please!" Toi cried out with a face covered in tears.

They made sure Amber was stable before they moved her. After taking her pulse and hooking her up to the oxygen machine, they put her in the ambulance.

Watching her lying there was almost surreal. This wasn't what we worked for. This wasn't how it was supposed to be.

Eventually, during the ride to the emergency room, she opened her eyes, but didn't move. I don't know if she was motionless because of embarrassment, or if she just didn't have the strength. I rode in the ambulance with her, while Toi waited for the police. I wanted her to know that we would be there for her.

At the hospital, the doctors assured me that Amber would be fine. I sat with her until she fell asleep, and then went back to her house to straighten up.

"What do you think happened Candice?" Toi asked.

"You know damn well what happened, it was that cock-sucka Randy! This time he's gone too far. Y'all my sisters and ain't no half-ass nigga gonna hurt my family."

With every piece of broken furniture I moved, I thought about how much I wanted Randy hurt. I wanted him to experience the pain that Amber was feeling. Have you ever hated someone so much that for a split second you would've killed them? Well, that's how I was feeling about punk Randy. I knew exactly what I needed to do to set things straight.

The one thing I learned growing up was that you always needed some thugged-out friends. Regardless how high you climb that ladder of success, sooner or later, somebody's gonna need a beat-down.

I called my friend Big Money. He knew something was wrong as soon as he heard my voice.

"What's the problem Sweet Red?"

I told him that I was fine, but I needed to speak with him.

"Cool, anything for you."

Red is what they called me back in my old neighborhood. Big Money was one of my childhood friends, turned hustler. He didn't have a formal education; he dropped out of school in the ninth grade, but he was intelligent. He knew the street game and made plenty of money playing it. Money ran the streets, didn't take no mess, and loved his Sweet Red. It was nothing sexual between us, but I gotta admit that I did screw him when we were teenagers. He is my nigga for life.

When we were growing up, I treated him with respect. You can say that he was a human version of that Biz Markie song, "The Vapors." Everybody jocked him now. When I left the hood and went to college, we kept in touch and remained close. There isn't anything that he won't do for me nor me for him.

Toi and I met with Money 'bout three hours later, on the east side at a park in Pleasant City. I told him about what happened.

"Money, I want that nigga Randy broke down. I mean Ike Turner, Rodney King beaten down. Hurt him baby. Hurt that nigga like he hurt Amber."

I knew if he couldn't take care of it, he knew someone who could.

He asked in a very serious tone, "Red, do you want him dead?" At that moment, Toi looked scared. She looked as if she didn't know how I was going to answer him. She had this expression on her face as though she was pleading with me to say no. Didn't she know that I didn't want to live with a man's blood on me for life?

"No, but I want that nigga to suffer. I want to watch that faggot get the shit beat out of him."

Toi was surprised by my response, but relieved. From that point, it was on. I knew that once Money walked away, I couldn't change my mind.

Life is like that. Sometimes the decision we make can affect a lifetime of events.

It's funny. I didn't have any second thoughts, at least not at that particular time. I told Toi that she could never mention this to Amber. I knew that Amber wouldn't agree. Even though Randy beats her like a dog, she still loves him.

I can't get wit' that program. I ain't Ja Rule, pain ain't love in my house.

As we were pulling off, Money drove alongside our car and asked if we wanted to have a few drinks. We agreed and followed him to a hole in the wall off Tamarind Avenue.

After my third drink, I was horny. What I really needed was a good eatin' out.

I leaned over to Toi. "Do you want to let Money eat our coochies?"

"Hell yeah," Toi replied, "as bad as I need a good screw right now, I just might give him some of this cat. Is he packing?"

"You'll be surprised," I said.

"Hey Money, let's go get a room and finish our drinks there. All this drama has worn me out."

"Where you wanna go Sweet Red?"

"Let's go to Trump Towers, next to the water on Flagler Avenue. I need somewhere I can order room service in the morning. I'm not trying to drive home tonight."

We followed Money to the hotel. When we got to the room, I went straight to the shower. The hot water running over my body helped me to relax some. I stood under the water for almost fifteen minutes before I decided that I had had enough.

When I walked out of the bathroom I said, "Money give me yo T-shirt, I don't want to put that dress back on." I had left my bloody clothes at Amber's house and put on one of her sundresses.

He took his shirt off and threw it to me.

His chest and stomach were defined to perfection. His chest was buffed with his perfectly protruded muscles, accented by beautiful small round nipples. His stomach was ridged with ripples and had a washboard firmness. I didn't remember Money looking so good. He was always fine, but he had gotten better with time.

Toi looked at him with lust in her eyes. She walked toward him and started rubbing his chest with her hands. Then, she bent over and started licking and sucking his nipples using her tongue ring. As she did this, he began to rub his rod, and it began to stick out, showing off the length and thickness through his pants. It looked like a throbbing bull trying to break out of its pen.

Toi touched it with her hand and said, "Damn, I have to see what you have in those pants." She began to pull his pants down, but he interrupted her and took off his pants and boxers.

Toi looked hungrily at his honey-colored eight-inch pole and started stroking it with her hand, then bent down and swallowed it. He sighed with excitement because I know he wasn't expecting that and neither was I.

Watching them got me hot, so I bent my knees upward, while lying on my back. I opened my legs so that Money could see and started rubbing my clit with my finger. I slowly dipped my fingers in my hole, leaned forward, and stuck them in Money's mouth.

"Taste me."

He sucked my fingers like they were lollipops. I pulled him down and pushed his head toward my dampened cat.

"Give me what I want." He pulled me to the end of the bed and started licking.

Toi lay down between his legs and kept sucking his glistening huge rod.

He opened my lips with his thumbs and started gently licking and teasing my clit. He flicked his tongue in and out of my hole as he continued to lick. Money had always sucked this cat good, but he had become a master.

Money maintained his usual vibratorlike pace until I came. DAMN!!! I came hard too. "Good gosh, I really needed that," I thought.

After I came, I pulled Money up and whispered in his ear, "Go take care of my girl, you know she wants you."

"Come here baby."

He started eating her out. Then, she pulled him up and said, "I can't wait. I want to feel it inside me." He jumped up and rammed his big cock inside her. She screamed, "Harder, harder, give it to me. Faster! Faster! Give me all you got!" The more she talked, the faster and harder he gave it to her. She had a smile on her face that let me know that she was enjoying every stroke.

By this time, the room was perfumed with the smell of sex. The ceiling fan wafted the aroma of lavender and natural musk through the air like a scented candle. The sound of Money plunging in and out of her seemed to get louder and louder until . . .

Toi yelled, "I want it from the back!"

Without hesitation, he picked her up and roughly turned her over on her stomach and pulled her fast and hard toward him. He then demanded, "Get on your knees, so I can give it all to you."

Okay, okay it started to seem a little too freaky for your girl, but they were having a good time.

Toi told me that a nut from the butt is more intense than a regular nut. I haven't experienced any backdoor action, but I won't say I never will.

For now though, my butt says exit only.

Their wild sexin' went on for hours. I fell asleep with sex sounds ringing in my ear.

I awoke with Money kissing me on my forehead. He stood fully dressed.

"Red, I gotta go take care my business." Then, he gave me a handful of hundred-dollar bills.

"Take care of the room and y'all room service. It's more than you need. If you need me, hit me up."

As he walked toward the door, he stopped and said, "Oh yeah, tell yo girl I said later, and the other thing will be taken care of." He went out the door without turning again.

I looked over at Toi. She was knocked out and snoring. If that Mandingo had given me that big piece of meat all night, I would still be out too.

FOUR

STOP!
Don't do it,
Let it go,
Remember . . .

you reap what you sow

The week following Amber's incident flew by quickly. Amber came home three days after she was admitted into the hospital. Once she was released, I suggested that she stay with me at my house until her strength was back up. She hesitantly agreed because she knew she wasn't ready to be alone.

Each time Toi and I tried to talk about what happened, Amber would say she didn't want to talk yet. She even tried to defend Randy by saying that she said something to piss him off. Every time I tried to comment, she would say, "Not now Candice. Please, I just need time." So me and Toi decided to wait until she was ready to tell us what happened. Eventually, she would come around. We never kept secrets from each other.

Over the years, we lied to our families, niggas, and anybody else, except each other. We were true sisters. The good, the bad, the ugly, we were still friends no matter what.

While Amber was at my house, we waited on her hand and foot. We cooked, massaged her, combed her hair, and called to check on her all day from work. Sometimes, I think that Amber was really enjoying the attention and the pampering a little too much. But she's my girl.

Four days after Amber came home, Toi and I decided to take her to Grandma's. We knew this would cheer her up, since Grandma's was one of our favorite places to just be us.

I could tell you so many stories about the three of us and that place. If those walls just had ears and mouths. . .

When we walked into the restaurant, everyone came up to Amber and greeted her.

"How you doing sweetie," said a gray-haired woman as she was walking out the door.

It's funny how news travels. The entire city was talking about how Amber was beaten up. It went from a robbery to a rape to a jealous boyfriend that had done it. Everybody made up their own story, and added a little more to it. But that's how it is in the hood. Street news is better than the eleven-o'clock coverage by a big network. It's 100 percent drama.

As soon as we sat down to order, my phone rang.

"Hello, this is Candice."

"Sweet Red, meet at Club Safari on Tamarind Avenue, at the far end of the parking lot, where the projects are. According to my man, Randy went to the club earlier inquiring about running it. The owner told him to come back at 9:30 tonight. You know how packed Club Safari is for happy hour on Fridays. So, Randy has to park at the far end of the lot.

"My people have been following him and now seems like the best time. It's 8:45, so we don't have a lot of time." In a low unsure voice, Money stated, "Red, this is what you wanted and now it's about to go down. When you pull in the parking lot, park, and do not get out the car. Once we start, just flash your lights when you think he's had enough."

"Had enough?" My stomach began to feel kinda queasy.

All of a sudden, my heart started beating fast. I tried to respond to what I had just been told, but I couldn't speak. After Money had finished talking, I just hung up the phone and prepared myself to do as instructed.

I tried to keep a straight face as I looked at Toi.

"Toi, that appointment we were waiting on is ready. We have to go now." I knew Toi was about to ask me what appointment, so I whispered Big Money in her ear before she could say anything.

"Right now? At this very minute? What are we going to do with Amber?" Toi asked in a shaky whisper.

"I hear y'all," Amber said thinking everything was some kind of joke or something.

"Nuh uuh honey, wherever y'all heifers going, I am going too."

I knew we didn't have time to debate with Amber, so in a very serious voice I replied, "No, you can't go, but it won't take us long. We can take you back to my house, or you can wait here and let Ruth entertain you for a little while."

Ruth is the waitress that has been working at Grandma's ever since we were in high school. She went to school with me, but didn't graduate. She looked at least ten years older than all of us. She has had a rough life.

Mocking a baby's voice, Amber said, "Well, since I can't go I'll wait here. Don't have me waiting all night though."

We drove to Club Safari in silence. Toi was shaking. You would think that somebody was about to kick her behind.

"Candice, you never cease to amaze me. You are so smart and pretty. Just looking at your innocent face, a person would never think that you would be down for something like this."

You damn right. I'm down for whatever. Whatever is right for me and mine.

"Well Toi, just call me an educated hoodrat who graduated from the streets. I moved out of the ghetto, but the ghetto ways are still in me. I know how to cover it up, but when your back's against the wall, you go back to what you know.

"Life is a cruel game, and if you're from the ghetto like us, then survival is one of your toughest opponents. Based on all that we've been through, we've learned from experience that only the strong survive."

FIVE

Watch out!!
Here comes the unknown,
It may bring joy or
It may leave you alone,
It could cause happiness, distress
Or something you can't detect,
But whatever happens, it's . . .

when you least expect

"Bummp, bummp!" Toi has to hear me blowing this horn. I called her fifteen minutes ago and told that wench we were on our way. Why she always keep a sista waiting?

After waiting for over ten minutes, she finally pranced out the house. "Y'all know better than to rush a diva."

When she walked toward the car, she began to strut like she was on a Paris runway. She stopped after every other step, posing, turning around slowly while lifting her arms in the air showing off her outfit.

"C'mon Tyra Stanks. We ain't got all day," I yelled under a playful laugh.

Toi was wearing blue pants that fit like a second layer of skin. Her shirt was black with blue paisley designs, and it hugged her upper torso. Her stomach was partially showing, revealing a tattoo around her navel that showed only by choice.

She bought that "Abs of Steel" video, and baby, it worked. Back in college, she always had a little baby fat around the waist, but Toi's all grown now.

I had to give it to her, she looked good. Toi didn't have any problems in the confidence area.

She got into the car being her talkative self. "I know I look and taste good tonight! I have my sweet body gel on and oh, let's not forget the FDS spray. Gotsta keep the poonanie smelling right. I might just let some lucky guy lick it." She rubbed her hand in her crotch and lifted it up to my face.

"Don't this coochie smell good."

"You are so nasty; don't put that mess in my face! I don't know what's been down there."

Amber interrupted the conversation, "I ain't trippin' neither. I could really go for some tonight. Girl, I need to be done up thug style, straight nasty."

On the way to the club, we joked and laughed about the last time we went out. It made me feel good to see Amber having fun again. It took her a while to get over the beat-down Randy gave her. But now things are finally getting back to normal.

It's been almost ten months since Randy's little, um . . . accident. He was released from the hospital after three days. He got just what he deserved, and I got what I asked for. You know, seeing Randy get busted up didn't make me feel better. I kinda felt sorry for him, lying on the ground bloody and helpless.

How I reacted to Amber's incident reminded me of what my mother used to always say: "Don't do things when you're mad because you may regret it. Bad decisions have haunting repercussions."

If I had really thought the whole thing over, I probably wouldn't have done what I did. It's too late for that now. What's done is done. Anyway, all I had to do was think about how I found Amber on the floor to convince myself that Randy deserved it.

It's a damn shame, but don't y'all know that Amber went flying to that nigga's bedside when she heard that he was in the hospital. By the time she arrived, his other women were arguing about who was staying, and whose man he really was.

"That's my nigga," one of the women yelled.

"Naw hoe, I got his baby right here in me," another stated while pointing to her swollen belly.

Instead of arguing with them, she left and decided to let him call her if he wanted to. Of course the nigga called, and she went running. She claims that she isn't messing around with him no more, but I know that's a lie. The one thing Amber couldn't do was fool me. But, that's her. The best I can do for her is to let her learn on her own.

When we got to the club, it was packed. "Damn, girl, what time is it?" Toi asked. It was still early, but the parking lot was full. It's good to have connections. When the valet runner saw me, he made room for my Benz up front.

"We got it goin' on, hey now," Amber said.

Inside the club, we could barely move. We had to push our way through the crowd. It was jam packed, wall to wall.

As we walked toward the bar, somebody rubbed my cat, then my butt. Damn, he really tried to get between my crack. I didn't bother looking around. If a nigga needed a cheap thrill that bad, let him have it.

The lights were extra dim; you couldn't see a thing. After squirming our way under a fluorescent beer sign, we noticed some paid-looking niggas by the pool tables. They were shooting pool and sipping on Moët. We headed over to where they were, but my song by Trick Daddy came on. I went right to the dance floor.

"Ladies, I'm feeling this crowd tonight." I pulled a guy standing next to me on the dance floor. The music, the crowd, the vibe, it was intense. Every beat from the music, pulsating through the huge speakers, ran through my body. At that moment, the music took over my body.

"Look at Miss Soul Train," Toi said to me.

"I know you don't think yo rhythmless behind can dance better than me." Joking with her, I said, "Girl, I choreo-graphed three music videos, remember."

"Yeah, in yo dreams."

Toi came to the floor dancing. She stopped, planted her feet, stuck her butt out, and started shaking her cheeks. Then, she went down to the ground slowly, with her legs spread open, and bounced a few times before she came back up.

"Ya mama taught me that, Candice."

"She learned it from yo granny, the original 'Solid Gold' dancer," I replied.

Amber soon joined in. We had gotten our groove on for years in the club. We swung our hips from left to right in a circular motion, from front to back, like we were hunching, and then dropped to the floor.

We were dancing for thirty minutes straight before we went to the bar. We ordered our usual, tequila shots.

"Six tequila shots with salt and lime please," I told the bartender.

"Six? What's up with that?" Amber said.

"Two each. What's wrong, you ain't hangin' tonight?" I asked Amber.

"Hell yeah I'm hangin', sex is always better when ya have a little buzz. Ya feel me."

We all grabbed our first shot, held our limes in our hand and I said, "You lick." We all licked the salt seductively from around the rim of the glass. "You swallow." We swallowed the shot down with one gulp. "And you suck." We sucked our lime and acted as if we just had an orgasm.

As Toi finished the second shot, she noticed a guy staring at her, licking his lips.

"Damn, I wish I was that lime and salt."

"Well, maybe you can be if you say the right thing and work with the right tools."

Toi was in rare form. She wanted to D, and she was definitely getting her freak on tonight.

I hear y'all broke nigga's hating in the background. "Why these hoes just freakin' every nigga in town? I bet they got every disease in the book. "

Well nigga, too bad, you just mad 'cause you can't get none. You'd be the first nigga in line if this coochie was laid out on a platter. Don't hate because we livin' large, in control and doing our own thang. You know, we got it going on, now what?

We have a chance to do what men have been doing since day one. A woman can pick a guy, screw him, and go. Men can finally get a taste of their own medicine. I ain't saying be a dog, but most men call you a bitch behind your back anyway. So, why not be the HBIC, head bitch in charge.

As we prepared to take another shot, three guys walked over. One looked at me and said, "I know you from somewhere."

"Where? I don't remember you."

"I know . . . the Essence Festival in New Orleans this past summer?"

"Yeah, I was there. All three of us went," I replied.

Then the nigga went left and said, "I thought I knew you. Remember, I got that stuff all night long. Don't you remember?"

Amber and Toi's faces frowned up. They both had that "I know this nigga didn't" expression. Now y'all already know.

I didn't hesitate to respond, because that nigga had me all messed up. I answered in a very soft and professional voice, "Well, if you would have said that you ate my cat all night long, I would've had to think about it. I know you didn't get to paradise because a man looking as broke as you are, wearing skintight Eddie Murphy Delirious pleather pants, surely can't afford this premium body or any of my valuable time. Anyway, your breath needs some help right now."

I placed a mint on the counter in front of where he was standing, then went back to sipping my drink. Amber and Toi, along with that fool's boys, burst out laughing. He just walked off and motioned for the other guys to follow.

When they left, Toi started sucking on a lime and licking her lips, silently flirting with the guy that had been looking at her. As I looked up to see his response, I saw a prospect. He looked sorta familiar; I could barely see with the dim lights.

I started squinting and moved a little away from the bar. I recognized that face. What was he doing there? I know that can't be Mike. The room was so dark it must've just been my imagination.

Oh my gosh, it is him! I can't believe it. Y'all remember Mike, my lover, for that one night.

I couldn't take my eyes off him. I watched his every move. He was looking good. He had on a pair of brown dress pants and a button-down shirt that showed off his broad shoulders. His hair was neatly twisted, and his diamond loop earrings could be seen from across the room. There's something about a polished-up street nigga that drives me insane.

I closed my eyes and took a deep breath. I remembered how good he felt and smelled. My heart started pounding fast, and I got nervous. "Calm down Candice, calm down," I started saying to myself. What was he doing in the club? I know he don't live in West Palm Beach, I been here most of my life. I thought he was a guest at the party where we met. I never asked though.

I wanted this man. Good gosh! I wanted this nigga, but I wasn't ready. I had no need for a relationship. I couldn't afford to fall in love. I wasn't ready to share my time, thoughts, or my whole self with a man.

My life was comfortable. I did what I wanted to when I wanted to. I wasn't gonna change for love or lust.

Damn, he saw me.

Here he came.

I waited for any distraction. As much as I wanted him, I couldn't talk to him. Good, someone tapped him on the shoulder.

I quickly blended into the crowd and proceeded to the restroom.

After sitting in a stall for what seemed like hours, I decided to go back to the bar. It was last call, and the lights were starting to come on. I saw Toi and Amber talking to the guy who she was flirting with earlier. Good. Mike's already gone.

"There go Lil Miss Shake It Fast," Toi said when she noticed me.

They started walking in my direction.

"Where have you been half of the night?" asked Amber.

"I was trying to find me a good tongue for the night." Everyone started laughing and headed toward the exit.

SIX

Life is unpredictable and usually unfair
It doesn't go as planned, so why do you care,
About the Love and Happiness that come
with so much pain,
One minute you're at peace the next
you're damn near insane,
Why are you here, is there a point
Can you ever have it all or . . .

whatever you want

I can't believe it's spring already. Work's been so hectic, I haven't had any time to see my girls. Owning Money Makers, a company that specializes in taxes and financial planning, has given me financial security, but it also takes up most of my time. Ever since I added another CPA, three accountants, and two personal managers, my business has doubled each quarter. By the end of the second fiscal year, profits had increased 300 percent.

One thing I've learned in this business is that people with money like to be pampered and those that don't have a lot of money like to be treated as if they do. It's like anything else; people don't like dealing with reality. It's just like being around street hustlers—investors act the same. The only difference is that their hustle is government sanctioned.

I decided to leave the office early today. Working fifteen-hour days over the past three months had taken its toll. I needed to relax and clear my mind. Sometimes we all need to get away for a minute or two. Life is way too short to spend all your time working.

Nevertheless, my friends and I have made our businesses three successes. Toi's marketing firm and Amber's health club bring in upscale clients and plenty of revenue. In other words, we ain't hurting for money.

Amber's health club caters to the elite. Some of my clients work out there, but most of them just use the massage and manicure services. The customers that get a chance to talk with Amber always ask her how she got into the business. You gotta admit, it's kinda unusual for a black woman to own a thriving health club with five-star service. But when you think about it, good service comes second nature to blacks. Our great-great-whatever had no choice but to work hard and be perfectionists. They never got the respect and money they were due, but we will.

Amber always tells the curious patrons about her good friend that helped her start by putting together a stellar business plan. She also says that her friend put her up on some good investments that brought her big returns. Since these people are usually money-hungry, they always listen attentively. Yeah, I know it's a hustle, but it works.

Most customers end up wanting to know who this friend is and if she can do something for them. Amber then gives them my name and number, and once they call, the rest is history.

What Amber fails to tell them is that I own 60 percent of her business. Well, I own it until she pays me back the money I loaned her. I know that we are friends and down like that, but I still had her sign the necessary legal documents.

I normally don't mix business and friendship. But since I take care of the books, I decided to help a sista out. Humph . . . I've been pleased with her hard work. If she keeps it up, she'll be able to buy me out in five years.

I'm glad to see Amber doing something positive with her life now. She had it rough growing up. Her father was a small-time dope dealer. He was killed when she was nine years old, and her mother, bless her heart, was a maid for a white family in Palm Beach. When Amber realized that a woman needed more than looks to survive, that's when she decided to apply for college. I'm lucky she did; I ain't know her as a kid. Her mom worked night and day so they could stay on the other side of town; not quite the hood, but not exactly the lap-of-luxury type of neighborhood.

Amber is an attractive woman. She's five-five with milk-chocolate-color skin, natural jet-black hair, and a small waist. She has an innocent look, but don't let that fool you. She can be very sneaky and deceptive, but she usually lets men take advantage of her.

Toi has been out of pocket since she's been seeing Johnny, the man she met at the club the last time we went out. Ms. Lady must be in love because she's devoted to him. And, baby, that is totally unlike her. He's a professional baseball player, but she meets men with money all the time. So, money surely wasn't the reason for her newly acquired relationship.

Me, I'd rather a businessman any day; their careers are

for life, unlike a ballplayer's. Most of those players don't even know what to do with their money when they get it. And an out-of-work athlete is the worst kind of nigga to have. All they do is whine. They want you to relive their glory days every time a game comes on. I ain't trying to sit up with nobody cosigning on bad choices for plays and calls.

My company represents a few professional athletes. They pay for advice, but never take it. All they want to know is how to get out of paying all of those taxes. You know, it's easy to make a million but hard as hell to keep it. Why do you think so many athletes are broke once their professional career is over? They spend every penny they make, don't save for the future, and then have the nerve to get mad when they have to give the Bentley back.

Toi has been trying to introduce me to Johnny's friend Fred, but I been too busy. Meeting some arrogant butthole is not my idea of a good time. I'm outgrowing that "ewwww ain't he fine" stage. A sista need a man, not a boy with money.

Maybe I'll call her when I get home and set something up for the weekend. She's not going anywhere without her man now, but that's the way it should be when you find a good person. Well, I guess I have to meet this Fred, for Toi's sake of course.

Toi was glad to hear from me. Although we hadn't seen each other lately, except for an occasional lunch, we still talked every day.

"So you got time for yo girl again," Toi said jokingly.

"Maybe I'll squeeze you in between my five o'clock and five-fifteen."

We both immediately burst into laughter. I had worked so much lately that I didn't have a chance to really smile at anything personal, much less laugh.

Knowing that I'd take some time off this weekend, I decided to go back to work to prepare for a meeting coming up next Tuesday.

Friday came quick. I was apprehensive about meeting Fred, and I hoped they didn't mind that Amber was coming. She had called me earlier crying about Randy again. He had been staying with her for the past two weeks. When she came home from work, she caught him screwing Shaniqua on the living-room floor. I had to invite her, even though I know Toi ain't gonna like it.

I can't say I feel too bad for her though. She knows what he's about, but keeps on going back. She's getting exactly what she wants, drama. Yeah, I think she's dumb as hell right about now, but I just couldn't leave her hangin'.

I picked Amber up, and we met Toi at the steakhouse in Palm Beach. Fred was fine as hell. He played for the Expos. He was talkative, but actually had something to say.

I didn't sweat him because Amber was with us. He didn't know either of us, he had the right to be interested in Amber if he wanted.

After dinner, we went to Club Safari, danced until three in the morning, and then went to Grandma's for breakfast. By this time, Fred was macking hard. He let it be known that he was interested in me, or should I say he wanted to go to bed with me.

He asked, "So, what are you doing later?"

Then he kinda smiled while licking his lips. You know, just like L.L. Cool J does.

"Going home and getting into my bed."

"Why don't you come with me, I'd like to spend some more time with you."

I guess I was supposed to jump for joy when he said that, since he played major league baseball, made twelve million a year and was sexier than a motha.

I asked in a rhetorical, but confident way, "Why should I go with you? There's nothing to do this time of night but screw, and I don't want to do that right now, not in the mood."

And I meant that. If we were gonna play games, you better believe we were gonna play by Candice's rules. Y'all feel me.

Still exuding confidence, he continued by saying, "Because I want to be with you, and I'm really enjoying your company."

Who did he think I was, a broke groupie? I knew what the nigga wanted, and that was the coochie. His confidence soon grew to cockiness, and this began to piss me off.

"Well, car note ain't due. House is paid for. Already paid my bills for the month. Ain't no malls open, so why would I want to go with you, unless you want to taste this sweet candy."

He looked at me in disbelief.

"Cool, if you sucking?"

"Uh, sorry sweetie. These lips ain't made for that."

"Well, what do I get out this deal?"

"Let's see . . . if you eat it and eat it good, I just might let you get inside me. But, it won't be tonight. I'm not going to play games with you because even if you taste it you still ain't getting it tonight."

He stared at me for a minute, trying to decide what to say. "You so damn sexy, I'll eat it. Yeah, I'll eat it if that's what really turns you on."

Now, I know a bullshitter when I see one. The nigga talked a good game, but he wasn't eating nothing. Well, that's okay, I was enjoying myself, and wasn't ready to go home yet.

"My girl has to come with me. Do you have a problem with that?"

He looked at me and then he looked at Amber.

"Hell naw, I don't mind. Let's get outta here."

I have to admit, Fred had it all. His neighborhood was beautiful. His home was between Palm Beach Gardens and Jupiter Beach in a subdivision with homes worth at the least seven hundred thousand dollars or more.

"This is nice," I said to Fred.

He just smiled and kept driving.

We went through a guarded gate and continued twisting and turning through streets. Each house we passed was custom designed with topiary on the perfectly manicured lawns.

We finally stopped in front of a gate that had the letters FG welded in the center of a black wrought-iron fence. The gate's opening was in the middle of the FG. We entered slowly and waited for Amber to follow. I rode with Fred and she followed us in my car. When she entered, the gate slowly shut.

We drove up the winding driveway to the front of the house. There was a beautiful waterfall in the center of the driveway. It was lit up with lights shining from underneath the water.

When I walked into the house, I knew this man had class.

"You have a very beautiful home," I stated.

He seemed a little embarrassed.

"Thank you."

He turned on a dome light that shone on a semicircular alcove in which several hand-painted African art pieces were aligned on shelves.

"Would you all like to sit in the den or the bedroom?" he asked.

Yeah right. What kind of bull was this nigga spitting? When have you ever heard of people chilling in a stranger's bedroom? Well, you probably thinking, "When do you hear of people doing most of the crazy things I do?" Shoot, you only live once.

"It doesn't matter, you decide."

Surprise, surprise . . . we followed him to the bedroom. Amber and I sat in the sitting area across from the bed.

"Make y'all self comfortable."

He slipped off his slacks and put on a warmup suit.

"Can I take a shower?" I asked. "I smell like smoke." He gave me a towel and walked me to the shower.

The shower was all marble with gold spigots in each corner. There was a bench with big fluffy embroidered towels on the rack outside the glass doors. The water was so soothing, massaging my sore muscles.

By the time I came out, Fred and Amber were lying across the bed. "Come relax," he said, as he patted his hand on the blanket next to him.

"Have you changed your sheets? I don't want to sit on anybody else's mess."

He laughed and said, "I don't have women to my house all the time, this is very unusual for me. My bed is clean. I don't like sleeping on nobody's mess either."

I lay across the bed.

"Turn on some music, please."

He got up and turned on the CD player and then went to his minibar. He pulled out a bottle of chilled Cristal. You know, I love a man with good taste.

I was wearing a jersey that he had given me when I got out of the shower. Amber had on her G-string panties and the shirt she wore out. "Oh, that's my song!" I said loudly as I got up and put on my heels. It was Michelle's "If."

I started moving seductively to the slow romantic beat. I began to rub my body and roll my hips in a circular motion. I looked deep into his eyes, grabbed his hands and held them while I sang the words to the song.

While I sang, I didn't take my eyes off him. I slowly turned my back, bent my knees and dropped down to the floor. I kept my hands around my ankles, and I stuck my butt straight in the air, revealing all of my private parts. I rubbed my hand up and down my inner legs, turned around and rubbed my perfectly round breast as I began to stand up. I blew him a kiss, and put my finger to my mouth to kiss it softly.

He couldn't take his eyes off me. He started rubbing on himself. When he tried to touch me, I popped his hand.

"Ungh, unghh . . . you can't touch the dancer. You know it's against the house rules."

The next song came on, "Nicety," that was a favorite of mine too. I kept dancing, losing myself more and more to the moment. You know when you get that natural high. That's how I was vibing at that time.

The champagne was really starting to get to me; I needed to lie down.

"Change the music and put on some Trick Daddy so we can give you a taste of the Rolex." The Rolex is a strip club in Miami.

Amber started dancing as soon as she heard the music. She started gyrating her hips in and out really fast. She turned around, bent over and slipped her G-string off. Fred's eyes got big as hell as she bent over, showing every inch of her big butt. She even opened her butt cheeks so that everything between her legs could be seen. Then she stood straight up and started shaking her butt, while barely moving her legs.

She grabbed Fred and said, "Let me see what you got."

He started dancing, and we starting yelling, "Take it off, take it off! Let us see what you working wit, take it off!"

I got up, pulled his boxers down but wasn't ready for what I saw. Amber and I looked at each other with the same "Damn his D big" look on our faces. I reached up and touched it to make sure that I wasn't seeing things. No pun intended. The harder he got, the bigger he got. Boy was this nigga huge. He had at least ten inches, and it was as fat as a cucumber. His daddy must've been a horse 'cause ain't too many men packin' like that.

Amber whispered in my ear, "I gotta get some of this. I want to see how that big thang feels inside me!"

"Do yo thang girl, or should I say do his."

She reached over and started stroking his pole. Then,

being the closet freak she is, she bent down and started lick-ing his dick head. As she began to suck him, he looked at me as if he was asking for permission.

I didn't mind because I didn't own him. For that matter, I didn't even know him. Don't get me wrong, the brotha had it going on, but he wasn't mine. That nigga could give it to whoever he wanted. Anyway, I didn't know if I wanted to see him again. I don't get excited over looks or size of the pole. A nigga got to get my mind first. If he can't do that, then a good screw is all he can give me.

I didn't want him to feel uncomfortable, so I leaned down and started kissing him on his neck. If he was waiting on my permission, I thought I'd better give it to him.

"Enjoy yourself, baby."

I think my calmness confused him. Even though I know he had no intention of stopping Amber, he still looked like a child stealing cookies from the cookie jar.

"Y'all have a good time," I whispered to him.

In order to give them some privacy, I turned over and began watching *The Five Heartbeats*. I just love old Eddie Ray King. I know y'all remember that scene. But y'all know I got a little freak in me too, so I had to peek at them. You know, to maybe get a few new positions or something.

Amber eventually stopped sucking on Fred. As she came up, she tried to put her cat in his face for some licking.

"I don't eat pussy."

Sure nigga, I thought, but I do like a man that doesn't eat every woman he screws.

Amber did not care if he ate the coot or not, she just wanted to feel that big piece of meat inside her.

He pushed her head back down so she could suck him some more. He said, "Yo lips feel so good around this dick, don't stop until I tell you to."

I thought to myself, "Nigga can't eat the coot but he want his D sucked."

Amber sucked that thang like she got a Master's in that field. She sucked it so good she made me horny. I know she was real horny by now because she went crazy on the dick head.

I didn't know whether Fred was just that smooth, tasted that good, or if Randy had beaten Amber to the point of retardation. 'Cause if a nigga can't eat this cat ain't no way he is gonna get a first-class head job like that.

Amber finally stopped sucking and then tried to sit on it without a rubber. Yep, Randy done knocked her screws loose. Raw D with a strange nigga, honey please. Thank goodness Fred told her to wait then reached in his night-stand to get a condom. I was impressed. Most men would've dove in naked head and all. Maybe Fred might be worth checking out a little more.

When Amber did sit on him, she stayed up there for over thirty minutes. He hit it from the back for about forty-five minutes. By the time they finished, the movie was at its last thirty minutes.

"Bet you never had a workout like that at spring training," I said jokingly to Fred.

After the movie ended, I jumped up and started putting on my clothes.

"I don't want you to go; please stay."

"But we . . . "

"Please."

"Yeah Candice, please," Amber added, mocking Fred.

I got back in bed and lay on one side as Amber lay on the other.

Although he had just boned the hell out my friend, he rolled to my side and put his arm around me. Amber didn't seem to care, she was already knocked out.

"Goodnight sexy," he softly said in my ear.

The turning point of misery
is knowing who you are,
Now deal with your troubles
no matter how close or how far,
You are strong, you can do anything,
The best is yet to come
So welcome your . . .

new beginnings

On Monday when I got to work, five dozen beautiful white roses were sitting on my desk. The card read, "Had a great time. Can we get together again, just you and I? Call me, Fred."

Well, well, well . . . looks like Fred really wants to get next to me. The flowers were nice. If a man takes time out of his day to not only think about you, but also send you flowers, then that's special.

"Excuse me. Ms. Candice, we have a meeting with our biggest client in fifteen."

My assistant had walked up next to me without my noticing.

"Okay, where's the file?"

The day went by fast, and I was so busy that I forgot to

call Fred. Like I keep saying, "Money first, fun later." I left work without even taking the roses.

I was exhausted by the time I got home. I lit my candles, turned off the lights, put on some slow jams and ran me a bubble bath. Just as I was surrendering to the hot water, my phone rang.

"Hello."

The bass-heavy voice on the other end said, "Hi Candice. Did I catch you at a bad time?"

I hesitated before I answered. I wanted to make sure it was Fred. Ya girl ain't bragging, but a player gon' play. Y'all stop hating, I hear ya. Not many people had my number and Fred wasn't one of them.

To make sure I didn't get caught up, I said, "Well, actually I'm in the tub."

"Would you like for me to call you later?"

Bingo, it's Fred. That's definitely his voice. Toi must've given him my numbers. Good looking out girl.

"No, I can talk. Thank you for the roses. They were beautiful. I'm sorry I didn't get a chance to call you back, but work was hectic."

"I know. I called to see if you wanted to go to lunch or something, but your secretary said you were in a meeting. But that's cool. So, when can I take you to lunch, dinner or maybe Paris?"

Okay Mr. Money Bags you have run up on the right sista now. I know you got money and I don't mind helping you spend some of it. "Okay dinner Friday, lunch tomorrow and Paris in the spring. Will that work for you?"

"Whatever you like," he answered.

"Well let's do lunch tomorrow, work on dinner for Friday and can confirm the rest later. Don't say something that you can't back up because I am looking for everything you tell me."

"I can back up everything that I say and then some," he replied confidently.

"Friday sounds good, but I will tell you definitely at lunch after I check my schedule. I might have to fly out of the country to check on a couple of my investments," I stated in a teasing voice.

"Do I have to wait until then to call you, or can I call you back later when you're relaxed in bed?"

There we go. See my sistas, no matter how much money a man has, the bottom line is that he's still a man. And, being a man, all he really wants is some ass and attention. When you act like they might get neither, they'll start begging like the hungry dogs most of them are.

I told him yes, and then hung up with no other words. You gotta keep them guessing. Not long after I got out of the tub, he called back.

"Candice?"

"No, this is Cindy, Candice's sister."

"Oh, I'm sorry. Is Candice there?"

"I'm just kidding, it's me. So, I see you don't recognize my voice. That's strike one."

"Hold up. You didn't warn me about your curve ball questions. Let's be fair and call that a ball."

"All right. Just this time."

I enjoyed his conversation, and as we talked, I started looking forward to seeing him.

There y'all go again. Why y'all keep getting all up in my business? How can I be catching feelings for a man who screwed my girl right in front of me? Because I can do that. Y'all need to gon' grow up. I know you don't think yo daddy was the first nigga yo mama boned. I'm about to do this damn thang, feel me.

When I arrived for work Tuesday morning, there was another arrangement of exotic flowers in a crystal vase.

"Don't forget about lunch today and dinner Friday. Missing you much," read the card. I told y'all a nigga'll step up his game if given the proper incentives.

I smiled as I read the card. My secretary, Ms. Debra, said, "From that smile, you must be missing him too."

I kept smiling and reviewed my "To Do" list for the day.

Ms. Debra is a sweet middle-aged woman, who is extremely efficient and effective. She takes good care of me, but she's a nosey old hag. She's like one of those friends of your mama who always has something to say about everything. But I wouldn't trade her in for nothing.

I had to call Fred to thank him for the gift. I didn't have his cell phone number on me, so I called his voice mail service.

"Hello Fred. Your gift was lovely. Keep it up, and we might have to go into extra innings. Oh, I'm sorry I have to cancel lunch today, but call me."

Fred called back right before lunch, and we talked until he had to go back to practice.

From then on, we talked every day, sometimes four times a day, until Friday. Toi called and said that she knew Fred was excited about the date. She overheard Johnny talking to him. If Toi was good for anything, it was snooping for information. She says that she know she is nosy and she can't help it, that it is in her blood. I think she went into the wrong field; she should've been a detective.

"So, Ms. I don't wanna meet Fred, are you going to give him some? I know you want to. You already know what he's working with. A thick big summer sausage."

"Nah, I ain't trying to go there. To make sure, I'm going to get under this water for a quick nut. I just need to relax a little. So I will call you back in a minute after I get this nut."

"Wait Candice, I am not finish talking to you yet."

"Either you gonna listen while I get this nut or I will call you back."

CLICK.

"I thought so."

I am trying to get this monkey off my back before I go out with this fine man tonight. Girls, ya'll know how it is when ya horny and have not had a nut in a while . . . you just might do anything to get the D, tongue, or whatever you need at that time. So I am gonna get mine right now and not worry about it later.

It took me less than a minute to come under the running water. Damn that was a good hard cum. Let me call Toi back before she start acting crazy.

As soon as she answered the phone I said, "Okay girl, I'm finished."

"I can't believe you. You would rather lie under some running water than get the real thing. Something is definitely wrong with you."

I replied, "The water never lets me down, it hit that clit

for as long as I want it to and I know it is going to be good every time."

"Why didn't you just let Fred take care of that situation? You already know what he workin' wit."

"I don't want it yet."

"Girl, stop fronting. Bet you can't remember the last time you had some meat in ya life."

"You right. You know I want to give it to him so bad, eww wee, but not tonight."

"Why?"

Someone knocked at the door.

"Gotta go, love ya."

It was Fred. He had a single white tulip in one hand and a bottle of perfume in the other. I ain't gon' lie, he caught me off guard. I wasn't expecting the flower. When we talked earlier in the week, he asked what my favorite flower was. I gave him a few hints, but never told him it was tulips. He got it right. Damn nigga, you showing some strong potential!

I told him to come in for a few minutes, so I could finish up some business.

"Your house is like you, flawless. I see you're into African art too," he said.

"Thank you. Yeah, I try to keep a little of the motherland around me. It keeps me grounded and thankful for what I have."

I gave him a bottle of Dom Perignon to open and asked him to pour me a glass too.

When I returned, he said, "Let's have a toast."

"To a wonderful evening and new beginnings."

As I looked into his eyes, I saw something that made my heart flutter. Suddenly I felt like a young girl on her first date, nervous and very apprehensive. Everything was almost unreal.

When we walked outside, a black Mercedes-Benz limo was waiting for us. A flask of my favorite drink mixture, Moët, Grand Marnier, and Alizé, was inside the limo. I'm weak for a man that not only talks to me, but also listens. I mean really listen to what I'm saying.

"So you're pulling out all the stops, I see. I like. I like."

"Well, special ladies deserve special things, and let's just leave it at that."

Now this is how a man is supposed to treat a lady.

The limo drove us to a restaurant on South Beach. They're supposed to have the best stone crab dishes in the city. After a delicious candlelit dinner, we went to a small sidewalk café on Ocean Boulevard.

We had drinks, talked and laughed. Then, we walked along the seawall and sat by the oceanfront. The moon was full and a slight breeze was blowing from the water. He held my hands as we talked. Every time he touched me, my heart would beat faster.

He was so different from what I expected. I thought he'd take me to eat and then just try to get the draws. I was definitely prepared to tell him no. I must admit, he surprised me with the perfume, the drinks, the restaurant, and the tulip. Oh, let's not forget the first-class ride; it's not every day that a man takes you out on your first date in a limo.

Fred seemed to be a gentle spirit. He was attentive, a good listener, and he complimented me all night. We took our shoes off and walked along the shore. It was a beautiful night, and it felt comforting to be with Fred.

Yeah, I know. This is the same nigga that had his thang halfway down my friend's throat. But, think about it. We all have skeletons in our closet. I just happen to know one of his; he's a freak. But y'all already know, sometimes I like a little freaky-deaky in my life too.

I guess he was thinking the same thing.

"Did it bother you to see me have sex with Amber?"

Even though I wasn't really tripping, I had to let him know that because he was not my man he could do whatever and whoever he wanted to, but if he was my man or we were working on a relationship it would not be tolerated.

Nevertheless, being who I am, I just looked at him and said, "Why should it bother me? I didn't know you at all back then. Don't get me wrong, if it happened again, I wouldn't give you the time of day. But, you ain't my man, so I can't tell you what to do."

Okay, okay. Believe it or not I really did not give a damn; actually I enjoyed watching him in action. I guess it's just the freak in me. Anyway, I have never been the kind of woman who stayed on dick patrol. A nigga gon' give it away every chance he gets, but he won't drive me crazy worrying about who gonna get it next. I don't know about you, but I'd rather know what a nigga been in before he all up in me. I gotta little change, but Magic's miracle cure ain't hit the market. If you know what I mean.

"Candice, I'd like to spend as much time with you as possible before spring training is over. I have to go to Montreal when the season starts. From the first time I saw you, I wanted you. You are one of the few women I've met that didn't mention a relationship, a man, or sex as a top priority. I realize that the other night complicates things, but I hope we get can past that. So, will you give me a chance?"

Well, at least he realized that whatever we were thinking about doing was going to be a difficult ride.

I couldn't do anything but smile and say, "I think I'd like that." He looked relieved as I snuggled up against him and lay my head on his shoulder. He felt like a big warm teddy bear in my arms during the limo ride back to my house.

We didn't say a word during the ride either. The only sound was the wind whistling and Keith Sweat playing in the CD player.

I can't lie, I fell asleep because it was so comfortable. But we did eventually make it to my house and my little Cinderella pumpkin ride was just about over.

"Wake up baby, we're here."

"I'm sorry. I didn't mean to doze off like that." I guess the long days I had been spending at work were finally catching up with me.

"It's fine. I like watching you sleep. The little drool coming out your mouth. The small little poots."

"Stop lying! Ewww . . . I'm so sorry."

"Gotcha. I'm just paying you back for the 'this is Cindy, her sister' joke. You looked like an angel; so peaceful, so beautiful."

"Stop making me blush."

After he opened the limo door, he walked me to my porch and asked, "Can I see you tomorrow? I'm leaving in five weeks, and I don't want to miss any chance to be with you."

"I don't know. Well, yes you can see me tomorrow. Would you like to come in for a while?" I wasn't ready for him to leave, so I added, "Go take care of the limousine driver, and I'll take you home later."

"Are you sure?"

"Yeah baby. I'm sure."

It was something about this man that had me going. I wanted to throw him to the floor and make love to him all night. One thing I've learned is that if you want sex and want it so bad that you'll do anything to get it, then it's just lust. But, if you want to make love and can wait, then that's working toward a real friendship. Since Fred still wanted to come in even though I think he knew he wasn't getting the draws, I was sure he wanted more too.

We watched movies and talked until sunrise. I forgot that I had some clients meeting me at the office Saturday morning. I was late getting to work because Fred didn't have to be to practice until 11:00. I cooked breakfast and brought it to him in bed. Before y'all think it, no we didn't make love that night. As a matter of fact, he didn't even try to kiss me.

Over the next five weeks, I was with Fred every day. He took me to work on the nights that I stayed at his house. My work days were long and tiring. I used that as an excuse not to go to Fred's games. I did not want anyone associating me with him until I was for sure he was the one. I was really enjoying the time we spent together. For the first time in a long time, I caught myself saying "we" more than "I."

He sent flowers, stuffed animals, and lots of French chocolates. We were having a beautiful time together. Although we didn't make love, we held each other constantly. He was my sweetheart; the kind of man a woman only dreams about. I kept telling myself that he was too good to be true.

Every day I went to work, I looked forward to seeing him and waking up in the morning with him next to me. Some nights we stayed at my house and others we stayed at his. Everything was as perfect as it could be, and the thought of him leaving me tomorrow made me sad. My heart hurt like I was losing my best friend.

He had really gotten to my inner soul. What I was feeling really scared me, but I wasn't going to let him go. I wanted him. I wanted all of him, but I couldn't let him know yet.

EIGHT

You have cried all night
Even walked in the rain,
contemplated suicide
And other crazy things,
Let him go before he
Drives you insane,
You may be alone
But at least there's . . .

no more pain

I talked to Fred every day over the last month, but I was still missing him more than I expected. We were together every day before he left, but that didn't help. Even though he'd been gone for only a month, it still seemed like forever.

Before he left, we held each other every night, all night, and enjoyed each other to the fullest. We hadn't made love yet, and boy do I miss that. Whoever said, "You can't miss what you never had," is a damn liar.

I guess we were having mind sex. You know . . . like when you get into a person's head and they get into yours. Remember that song that said "you don't have to take your clothes off to have a good time." It was definitely coming to life here.

Fred wanted me to go with him when he left, but I have responsibilities, not to mention that I have a business to run. I think he tried to understand, but I could tell that he was disappointed. This was a man who was used to women dropping everything just to be with him.

Believe me, I had no intention of throwing everything I built away for love. Yo girl wasn't that sprung and anyway, love is too unpredictable. I let him know that I was going to miss him and even threw in a few tears. No matter how hard a man is, a pretty woman crying will bring him to his knees in a hot second. Being the diva that I am, when I play I expect to win, by any means necessary.

He even began calling me no later than thirty minutes after I got home from work each day. On that particular day, I knew that he would be calling a little earlier, as he had a meeting with his agent at our usual talk time. Not long after I walked into the house, the phone started ringing. I put down my briefcase and ran toward my bedroom. Shoot, it stopped before I could get to it. Although all I had to do was call his cell phone back, I decided to listen to the message. If I tell you this man's voice could make Martha Stewart wet, I'd still be doing him an injustice. As I pressed the play button, I heard Amber's voice.

"Candice, I did it. He finally pushed me too far, and I did it. Please come over because I don't know what to do," she said in an unusually calm tone.

There was an unfamiliar emptiness in her words. I knew she was talking about Randy. Maybe she finally left the nigga. It's about time cause the "get beat down boo hoo routine" was getting kinda old.

I called her right back.

"What's up girl? I know how you feel, but it's about time you left that sorry Negro." Knowing that she usually would burst into tears right about this time, I tried to make her laugh.

"You know that you were too much woman or should I say your coochie was too big for those three inches. You need a man that can fill you up not tease you."

When she did not laugh, I knew that something was wrong, because she was still serious. I didn't know what else to say until she started slowly speaking. "No Candice. I did it. He made me do it. He was in my bed, my bed with that hoe Shaniqua. I just couldn't take it no more. She had an apartment, why couldn't they just go there? Why my house? Why did he have to bring that whore in my house? Please Lord forgive me! I came home and saw her car in my garage. I could just see them laughing at me behind my back. Eating my food. Drinking up my wine. I am tired of being his fool. I don't deserve to be walked over and mistreated, I am too good to him. So, I went upstairs and heard them giggling in my bedroom. Can't you just see 'em Candice? She was all wrapped up in my Ralph Lauren sheets. I tried to hold it in. I stood there for a minute, with tears in my eyes, all torn up inside. Then I cracked open the bedroom door. I saw her riding him with a smile on her face and I just lost it. I can still hear her, 'oh daddy, daddy it feels so good.' I closed the door and went to the hall closet and got the gun. All I wanted to do was scare them and make them get out of my bed, out of my house. I put the gun in my purse and opened the door to tell them to get the hell out of my house. They just looked up and started laughing. Do you know how I felt? Why did they have to laugh at me? Why? He even said, 'Wait till I get this nut, I'm about to cum.' She laughed and kept riding him; bouncing up and down harder and harder while smiling at me. I felt so disrespected and violated when he told me to wait. How could he do that to me in my home, in my bed? I totally lost it, my mind went blank and my whole body went numb. I don't know what happened. I just snapped. I . . . I pulled the trigger."

"You did what, you did what, Amber?" I replied quickly.

"I pulled the trigger," she said slowly in a babylike tone as if she was unsure of what she was saying and what she had done.

I was speechless. I stood for a minute to collect my thoughts and made absolutely sure that she had said what I thought she said.

"Baby, did you shoot them? Amber, please tell me you didn't shoot them."

"I killed those mothafuckas. I killed them, both of them. I shot her in the chest, and I put a bullet in his nuts."

She sounded confused, but sure of what she was saying.

"Amber, listen . . . where are they now? Where are they now? Are they breathing?"

"I don't know. But, why they still smiling at me Candice? Make 'em stop! Please make 'em stop!"

She started crying and screaming, "Please Candice, make them stop looking at me, please, please, make them stop."

BAM!!! BAM!!! I heard two shots being fired in the background.

"Amber, what was that?"

She had definitely lost her freakin' mind, but she's my friend. I knew I had to keep her on the phone while I headed to her house. I got my cell phone out and called her.

"Answer the other line Amber, it's me. My phone is going out."

Y'all don't know how hard it was for me not to call the police. I ain't do nothing. Why am I even getting involved? This girl needs help. Would she do the same for me?

Yeah . . . yeah she would, without question. I had to help her the best I could, even if it meant losing it all.

As I talked to her on one line, I called Big Money on my business cell.

"Money!"

"Red? Is that you?"

"Meet me at Amber's house?"

"Who?"

"Money, please! Just meet me at Amber's house. Do you remember where she lives?"

"Yes, I do. What's . . ."

I cut him off and said, "Just come now, I need you."

I hung up. I didn't want to say too much over the phone. Call me paranoid or whatever, but I ain't with taking unnecessary chances.

When I got to Amber's house, her garage door was still up. I went in and closed it, so no one would notice Shaniqua's car. I went upstairs and found Amber in the bedroom saying, "You better stop looking at me, stop looking at me!"

She was still pulling the trigger, but she had used all the bullets.

"Amber! Stop it! You gotta get yo self together. You're in a lot of trouble sweetheart. Don't you know what you've done?"

She just sat there with soulless eyes and a jokerlike smile.

"Candice, I took care of those bastards. I told them that they better not come back," she said while rocking back and forth. She had definitely lost her freakin' mind.

I had to get her out of the room away from them. Hopefully, that would help her snap back to reality and realize what she had done. I took her downstairs and told her to wait for Money. I went back upstairs and found the gun. I put it in my purse. I couldn't trust that with nobody. I took a blanket and laid it over their bodies, and I started cleaning up the blood the best I could.

"Skreeeech!!!"

I heard a car pull into the driveway. When I looked out the window, I saw Money and his boy Black getting out of the car. I met them at the front door.

"What's the deal, Re —"

I cut him off, grabbed his arm, and told Black to wait with Amber. I took Money upstairs.

When we walked into the room, he saw the blood and said, "Damn baby, what y'all do? Kill a muthafucka?"

"Wasn't no y'all in this, Money. Amber did. She killed Randy."

"Ain't that the same nigga we beat down for y'all? Don't look like playboy doing too good. Got damn, she shot that nigga nuts off! Damn Red, she really messed them up. Yo girl has gone crazy in this motha!" he said with a semismile on his face.

"This ain't funny. They dead. She need yo help Money."

"Hold up Red, I'll take a bullet for you. Shit, you already know that I'll kill a nigga if they fuck with you. But you asking me to do a lot for ya girl. It ain't even much like that wit me and her."

"Baby, I have to look out for my investment; no, our investment. You know she run the club, and if she goes down, what's going to happen to our money? She owes me too much. I can't take a loss like that yet. You helped me get the money, so what about your interest?"

"Red, I don't give a damn about that money and you know that. Come on now. I taught you the street game. You already set me up so I can be legit. I don't need the streets no more. I still hustle 'cause it's in my blood, and that's all I know. I love what I do, and I love you too. If you want me to take care of this mess, I will; but not because of the money. Because you asked me to do it for you and you know that I'm yo nigga for life and I love you."

He looked toward the hallway and yelled, "Black, get up here now nigga." He asked me where the cars were. Then, he told me to leave with Amber and not come back for a few days. I took Amber and did what he said.

"Let's go Amber. Now!"

I packed Amber some clothes and headed to my house, but, for some reason, I kept driving.

I wasn't nervous. I just needed to think . . . you know, clear my head. I knew that Money would take care of everything. We'd been tight since childhood, but in ninth grade I put him up on some information that saved his butt back then. I told him he didn't owe me a thing, but he didn't see things like that.

It had to be fifteen years ago when I went to the movies with one of the OGs who ran the north side of Tamarind Avenue, Gangster D. That night, after the movies, we went to one of his dope spots to collect some money from one of his runners. He didn't know me and Money was cool, in fact no one knew. We kept our friendship on the downlow.

Money always thought that if anyone knew he cared for me they'd use it against him. He used to say that I was the only good thing in his life. He knew I wasn't like all the other girls.

Anyway, I heard Gangster D and his people talking about some dude that they were going to set up and kill. They said that the boy they were going to kill wouldn't know what hit him because they had a deal set up with him the next day.

On the way to the car, Gangster D said to his boy, "Don't forget to call that lil bitch Money and make sure the nigga still coming tomorrow."

When he said that, my heart dropped. Money was my boy. He ran the streets, but he wasn't a cold-blooded killer. Gangster D was known to shoot a nigga just because he was a few dollars short or if his dope was off by a dime bag. Even if an out-of-town nigga sold from what he called his blocks, he'd mess him up big-time. I knew I had to warn Money as soon as I could.

Now Gangster D wasn't the kind of nigga that took no for an answer. When he decided he wanted to screw you, he was going to get it, even if he had to take it. I knew he was like that, so I was already prepared to deal with him. I never planned to go to bed with him. I just wanted a free meal.

In the middle of dinner I said, "Ohhh, my stomach is crampin' so bad. Oh damn! It's hurting."

He said, "Let's go to my place. Once I give you this monster, you'll feel better."

"First, can you take me to the store, because I'm out of pads? My period's on, and I'm bleeding heavy."

"Damn hoe, I wanna get my stick wet, but I ain't into all that blood shit."

"I'm sorry baby, but I didn't know it was coming."

He took me by the store and then home. Before he drove off, he said, "I'ma get that the next time, so you better be ready when you stop bleeding. I'm tired of hearing all those damn excuses."

I went into the house and called Big Money.

"Damn! No answer."

I looked for him on every corner, but still didn't see the nigga. The only other place I thought he'd be was the motel on Forty-fifth Street. I knew he went there when he had one of his hoes with him.

His car was parked in front of room 121, but I knew Money. He wouldn't park in front of the room he was in. I knocked on so many doors that the manager threatened to call the police. Just as I was about to leave, I saw a curtain pull back.

"Money! It's Red. Money please, my mom is sick. I need you to take me to the hospital."

He opened the room door and came out in his draws. I whispered in his ear, "I have something important to tell you. Meet me at yo boy's house in Boynton. I need to talk to you, it's very important."

Money knew that I don't play games.

"Red what's wrong? Is yo mom okay?"

"Yeah nigga, but you ain't. Don't even tell yo girl in there that it's me out here."

"Don't worry 'bout her. She so high, she don't even know where she at."

Money left lil mama knocked out in the room and followed me. This was probably the scariest moment in my life, until now. I thought that Gangster D might see me and kill both of us.

When we got to his boy's place, I went through the front door and he slipped in through a back door.

"Look Money, do you have some business with Gangster D tomorrow?"

"How you know about that?"

"That don't matter, just listen."

I told him everything I overheard.

"Are you sure Red? I done some business with that nigga before."

"I'm telling you what I heard."

"Go home Red, and don't be hangin' out for a minute."

Later that week, they found Gangster D shot twice in the head with two of his boys. Their bullet-riddled bodies were left in the park in Pleasant City.

Nobody was really looking for who did it. Gangster D was a crazy nigga. He killed his own brother because he thought he disrespected him by smoking his rocks and not paying for them. Yeah . . . that nigga was as screwed-up as they come.

Money, on the other hand, was a real nigga. He didn't let nobody push him around, but he was respectful. He'd kill a nigga if he had to, but he'd let you make it if he thought you got the message.

After that, Big Money always watched out for me. If I had any problems with anyone, he took care of it. He made all the niggas on the street respect me; he treated me more like a best friend with benefits.

Amber and I ended up driving all the way to South Beach. We checked in at the Eden Roc Hotel. I had to call the office the next morning to tell them that I'd be in late, and to cancel my morning appointments. They didn't need to know that I was in Miami. Later, I'd call them back to say that I'd be out for a few days.

Amber slept for the first three days without saying or eating much. The only time she got up was to use the bathroom. She seemed to be in a state of delayed shock or something. I couldn't . . . no I didn't want to imagine what was going through her mind right then. I mean . . . she took two human lives. That had to be tearing her up on the inside.

By the fourth day, she just started crying out the blue. She cried until she had to throw up. Whatever was taking place in her head was finally starting to show. I ain't know what to do.

I just put my arms around her and held her tight.

"Just let it out. Everything's gonna be okay. Let it all out now 'cause when we get back to West Palm none of this ever happened. It's just a dream, a bad dream."

She caught me off guard with the first words she had spoken in days.

"I can't. I can't pretend like nothing has happened. I'm a murderer Candice."

I had to be firm with her so she would understand what the repercussions would be for the crime she had committed.

"Damn, Amber, are you crazy? Do you want to be some

woman's hoe in prison? You better learn to pretend like a motherfucka. Now, if anybody ask where you've been, tell them with yo new man at the beach. When somebody ask you about Randy, just say that you ain't seen the nigga in a while. They'll think he's laying up with another one of his women. No one should ask you about Shaniqua, but if they do, just say you don't really know her. Can you do that Amber? You have to do that if you don't want to be locked up for the rest of your life."

Silence took over the room. Neither Amber nor I spoke for hours. I just sat next to her holding her while she lay her head on my shoulder. I guess she was thinking about what I had just said to her.

She broke the silence with, "Thank you Candice. I don't know what I'd do without you." She lay down and continued to cry for the rest of the day.

The following morning, she woke up with a new attitude and a new spirit. She wanted to get out of the room and do something. She wasn't crying anymore; actually she looked damn good considering what she had just been through.

We ate breakfast at the poolside café. We made appointments to get massages and facials. I thought that would be good for her—you know, to help her relieve all the tension that had built up over the last week. I wanted to go back to our normal lives as soon as possible. All this was just way too much, but it was worth it if it meant helping out my friend.

I finally called Toi and told her that Amber and I drove to Miami to meet with some people about the club.

"Why ain't y'all hoes call me? Just because I got a man don't mean I can't roll. Speaking of a man, Fred's been trying to reach you."

So much had happened, I'd forgotten all about Fred this past week.

I didn't mention anything to Toi about the murders. She's a little too timid for this kind of situation. She damn near shitted when Randy got beat down. I don't know what she'd do if she knew Amber killed Randy and Shaniqua. She will never find out from me, it will be our secrets, Amber's and mine. Oh, I almost forgot about Big Money and Black.

I told her we'd be back soon and made a mental note to call Fred. I couldn't call him yet.

I was still trying to figure some things out myself. When I thought we'd collected ourselves enough, I told Amber to pack her clothes up.

The drive out here seemed more like a dream. Amber all zoned out and me . . . I wasn't all together myself. But the ride back was gonna be different, we were refreshed and recharged. As far as I was concerned, nothing had happened.

But when I really think about the whole ordeal, I can't lie to y'all. I can't help but think that I may have made a huge mistake. Yeah, I'm Amber's friend, but she killed two people. That just makes you think, hunghh? How well do we really know people or how well do you know them when their back's up against a wall?

After eight days in Miami, it was time to get back to reality, face the world and deal with what happened the best way we could.

"Come on girl, let's go. I want to get back before it gets too dark." And we were off with those last words.

I play to win
So don't cross me
Because I can
Be . . .

low down and dirty

Three months passed since I'd seen Fred. Although we still talked on the phone almost every day, it was time to get what I needed, some lovin'. I missed him, and I was ready to make love. I guess my body needed to validate the feelings my heart was submitting to. God, I hoped it was worth all the waiting. Just because he screwed Amber like a horny stallion didn't mean he'd exactly hit my spot. Women, we all have been there before. You hold out, waiting for a mental connection, and the sex turns out to be horrible. But I don't think it's gonna be like that with my baby, or will it?

To get the lovin' and answers I wanted, Toi and I decided to meet up with Fred and Johnny in Atlanta. Fred's team was playing Johnny's team in Atlanta. From Atlanta I was going back to Montreal with Fred for a week, and Toi was staying in Atlanta with Johnny. The way they were groping each other she might not go back home at all.

I decided to wait until we got to Montreal before we took

things to that next level. I wanted to tease him and work up his appetite in Atlanta. It's a well-known fact that keeping a man's D hard without letting him cum builds up his stamina. That is, if you can keep the nigga from jacking off in the shower.

But, I know what y'all really want to know is, "What's up with Amber?" She was getting better each day. At least she was going back to her normal routine. After we left South Beach, she never mentioned what happened that day. When we first got back, she put her house up for sale. You know, to try and distance herself from the whole ordeal. After the house finally sold, she bought a condominium in Wellington. Ms. Lady even started dating her marketing manager from the club. He was always interested in her, but she didn't want to push the issue since she was his boss.

He happened to see her at Grandma's a month or so ago. One thing led to another and they'd been inseparable since. I was happy for my girl. She finally had a man that appreciated her and who wanted a real relationship.

In Atlanta, the only time I saw Toi was when we rode to the ballpark. Time seemed to move so fast that we only ate with each other once during the trip. I didn't stay with Fred in Atlanta. I couldn't trust myself. Y'all know how it gets when you ain't had none in a minute. All he had to do was breathe hard enough and my panties would've been on the floor.

To my surprise, Fred didn't push the issue. Either he respected the hell out of me or had a little freak on the side. I told you he is a good man, but a man nonetheless.

He had to fly back to Montreal with the team. I hated going through Customs because the lines were always long.

A limousine picked me up from the airport and took me to a hotel. I thought that I was staying with Fred at his place, but he had other plans.

Ladies, this could be the one.

After I checked into the hotel, I sat at the bar to have a drink. I drank a couple of Grand Marniers mixed with Baileys. I was feeling pretty good and warm inside. I decided to go to my room and get ready for my nigga's big sausage.

When I walked into the room, I poured me a glass of red wine. No . . . haters, I'm not a drunk. I just wanted to be fully relaxed. It's been a minute since somebody's hit this. And damn, I needed to loosen my muscles. Fred's stick was unbelievably thick. Fellas, forget about that "size don't matter" bull. The bigger the mutha, the better.

I had to be good and damp before Fred's manhood got in me. I even brought some KY Jelly, just in case. Ya girl don't need her cat all cut up, swollen, and sore.

I could feel his moist tongue on my clit; those soft lips teasing my inner thigh. I was getting wet just thinking about it.

Here's another note for the men: Take the time to get the coochie wet. It may feel the same to you, but a woman will give you a lot more if she's into it. A fat thang ramming in and out of a dry hole ain't no sane woman's idea of a good time. That's enough talking with y'all, let me get back to getting ready.

I put on Betty's CD, lit some candles, poured me another glass of wine, turned the lights off, and then took a long bubble bath.

"Tonight's the night that Fred makes me his woman."

Betty Wright, I know exactly what you meant girl.

I couldn't wait for Fred to get there. Before I knew it, I found myself rubbing my clit, but I stopped because I wanted the real thing tonight.

Fred had to go to the park to get his car and luggage, then he would be right over. He said that he wanted to hold me and make love to me all night long. I was going to make sure that he did just that. After all my hard work, it was time to do what needed to be done.

As soon as I got out the tub, he knocked on the door.

"Here I come lover."

I put on a quick splash of my sweet-smelling body spray, and slipped on a sexy body dress with a pair of high-heel stilettos. We were about to get our freak on proper like.

I walk to the door.

"I've been waiting for . . ."

When I opened the door I was greeted by a woman, instead of Fred. She was around five feet four inches, very pale and kinda chubby.

"Are you waiting on Fred?" she said with tears rolling down her cheeks.

"Yes I am, and who are you?"

"I'm his wife."

The only thing that was missing from this moment was that "Dum Dunna Dun" music from those drama movies. And the only thing I could think of at this moment was "Why me?" It just seems like a girl can't win for losing.

She reached into her purse and pulled out a family picture with Fred, his wife, two boys around eleven and nine, and a little girl.

Not only does this trifling lying nigga have a wife, he has children. I can't hate on him for wanting to do his little freaky thing, but I couldn't believe he'd lie and pretend like he was riding solo. Girl, a nigga ain't 'bout a dime and you girl almost fell for the okydote. Now I understand why I am in a hotel room and not at his house. Damn, I'm glad I did not take him to paradise.

I'd never thought he was married, but, then again, I never asked. I just assumed, with all the time we spent together, that there was no one serious in his life. I guess that old saying about assuming stuff is true.

"I am so sorry. He never told me he was married."

She stood there with tears in her eyes.

"He always does this to me, but it was different with you. He even called you from the house when I was home. He didn't know I was listening. I think he might be in love with you."

"Look, I'm sorry. I don't mess around with married men. If I'd known he was married it never would have gone this far. You don't have to worry about me interfering in your marriage."

She started telling me about all of the stuff he was doing, to make sure I didn't want to see him again. Believe me, she did not have to convince me to leave her husband alone. I was out of there. Good thing I didn't unpack.

Y'all probably think I got exactly what I deserved. But what did I ever do? I know I'm no angel, but I haven't done anybody like this. This is messed up all around.

On my way to the airport, I called for a flight back to West Palm Beach. If I wanted to leave Montreal tonight, I had to fly to Philadelphia to change planes in Atlanta. I had to stay overnight there because I knew I would miss the connecting flight.

When I got to the airport, Fred called. I got to give it to him, this nigga had balls. I hung up in his face. He kept calling, so I turned off my phone. The sound of his voice made me sick. It's funny. I was more disappointed than hurt. Just when you think you've found a decent nigga, they always do some dumb junk that bring you back to reality.

This is exactly why I live the way I do. See, if I had gotten myself all caught up, you know, depending on a nigga, I'd be assed out. That's why yo girl always put business first and everything else will fall into place.

All right, all right, I did listen to one of his messages. Just to see exactly what the nigga had to say, for future reference only.

"Candice please. Please baby, don't do this to me. Don't do this to us. Please don't leave. I need to talk to you. Give me a chance to explain."

Exactly what was this nigga gon' explain? Explain that he is married and forgot to tell me? There was nothing that he could tell me or explain to me. I think that's what's wrong with most men. They think they can fix everything. But when you mess up, you just mess up, plain and simple.

Some of y'all might think I got played, but hell, that's life. Sooner or later all of us get fucked. You just have to know how to grease it up so it won't be so painful. The true player thing is to just go on, don't regret what happened, and learn from it. I can't hate the player. I just play the game.

The people that he owed an explanation to were his family. No matter if I live to be a hundred, I'll never understand how a man can turn his back on his own children for what he thinks is better. Fellas, if you want to impress the ladies, handle yo business. Women like men who are responsible and honest, sorta like a Cliff Huxtable type. Y'all can save all that big pimpin' for the rap videos.

I made it through customs just in time to catch my flight to Philadelphia. The airlines didn't have a direct flight to West Palm Beach after six in the evening. I had to fly to Philadelphia, then to Atlanta, and lay over in Atlanta until the morning. I just wanted to get away from Fred; I didn't care how many planes I had to change. On the plane, all I thought about was that this nigga was married. He was kind and gentle, but when it came down to it, he was a no-good nigga just like my ex-husband. Yeah, you heard me right. I got married my last year in college. It only lasted six months, but I still got very hurt from the ordeal. His name was Dante, and I dated Dante for five years. We spent all our free time together. We practically lived together. We decided to get married my last year of school. At the time, I thought it was the best move for me. He had finished school two years before me and went to work for his father. They owned a chain of five-star restaurants.

I knew he had other women. I didn't worry about it though. The way I figured it, all men mess around. It only becomes a problem when the nigga gets disrespectful.

Yeah, I was really young back then. People say women mature faster than men, so I can only imagine what dudes my age were thinking about life back then.

Like most niggas, my ex had to go get ignorant with it: Whores calling and hanging up, writing me letters and thangs. I had to leave.

Self-respect is all a woman has and when that is taken away, there's nothing else. Remember, with or without money, self-respect is more important than anything.

Dante was a hard man to deal with. I was one of the very few people who understood him. The main woman he was messing around with was probably thinking, "Yeah high-yella heifer, I took your man." I bet she really thought she was getting something. See, what most of these on-the-side hoes don't know is that it's easy loving someone else's husband, but when he's yours it's a whole different ballgame.

See, when you loving another woman's man, you don't have to deal with all the problems that go along with him. When he sees you, he wants to be bothered. But, think about when he don't want to be bothered, and you have to be there anyway. What happens when you have to deal with all his bull? When things don't go right, he takes it all out on you.

When you are loving another woman's husband, you don't have to deal with all that. You are not there long enough to deal with nothing. In fact, you really don't know him, and he really doesn't know you. What's going to happen when you are forced to deal with each other? Oh but yes, that's when it'll really hit the fan, and there'll be more funk than a George Clinton concert.

What about when he gets tired of you and goes to another woman? It's bound to happen, believe that! You see, dogs like to do two things, roam and fuck. And in the back of yo mind, you will always be thinking that, because you know how you got him. I definitely don't need that kind of stress. I can't deal with all that mind tripping.

He married his mistress. They stayed together for three

years and had two babies. From the moment I left, he's been knocking my door down. He didn't ever think that I'd leave, because of the money. I guess he never really knew me. Like that Street Team song say, "My life's been a struggle/ I was born to hustle/ I guess it's just my momma in me."

When we first broke up, I was hurt and brokenhearted. I even briefly entertained the thought of going back. I didn't know if I was going to make it. But, when your back's against the wall, you can either submit or come out swinging. Let's just say I'm not the submissive type.

Six months after he married her, he was trying to see me again. He didn't appreciate me until I was gone. He realized that the woman he married wasn't half the woman I am. She was lazy, nagged all the time, didn't have any class, and was very insecure about their relationship. She knew how she got him and that sooner or later he would start tippin' again. When he was gone a long time, she would drive by my place looking for him. She asked for him, and she got every part of that lowdown, no-good, "ain't made me bust a nut yet" nigga.

He kept trying to mess around with me, but I wasn't interested. When I was with him, the sex wasn't good anyway. He was too selfish in bed. I remember one night we got in bed and I knew he was horny. I reached over and touched his D. It was rock hard, so I sucked him off real good. I even swallowed the cum. Stop hatin', we were married, and men love that shit. Now, you would expect sometimes the nigga would return the favor, but twenty-nine out of thirty he just went to sleep. I had to play with my own cat. Now ain't that a mess, playing with yo cat while yo man sleep next to ya.

Another thing that was messed up, I couldn't even tell him what I wanted in bed. If I tried, he'd get mad and say something stupid like, "Who you been wit? Where you learned all that?"

Eww, that man used to make me so mad. If it wasn't for my personal massager, ladies y'all know what I'm talking about, I would've probably never got a nut.

I don't have any bedroom inhibitions, so I didn't understand why I couldn't be his whore and his wife. When a woman is down for you like that, it doesn't mean you have free rein over her. Too many niggas ruin perfectly good relationships by not recognizing that their woman only does freaky stuff for them, not because she just likes it. Don't get me wrong, there are plenty of nymphos out there, but most women aren't. They just want to give their man everything he could possibly want, emotionally and physically.

Now you can see why I don't want the problems that come with a married man, and I definitely didn't want one leaving his wife for me. I know I'd never be able to trust him. This was why I left Fred, and knew I'd never see him again.

On my layover in Atlanta, I called Toi and told her what happened. She couldn't believe it. She said Johnny never mentioned that Fred was married. Yeah right, that nigga knew. He was probably married too. Ain't no telling.

I told her I would be leaving in the morning, but she talked me into staying a few days. Since I had already planned to be gone from work for a week, it was not hard to convince me. Anyway, I need some friendly company right then and I knew Toi, being her crazy self, would accommodate me.

The next morning, I went to the spa and got a good work-out and massage. I took it easy for the rest of the day. I told Toi I would see her tomorrow. I wasn't up for company or conversation, just needed to get my thoughts in order, that's why I would not stay at Johnny's house with Toi when she asked me to.

I kept my phone off because Fred would not stop calling. It got to the point where I just wanted to cuss him out and tell him to leave me alone.

The next day Toi and I went to lunch. She said that we were going out tonight and she wouldn't take no for an answer. Johnny and Toi would pick me up for dinner and then dancing at Club 120. This scene was all too familiar. This was how it all started with Fred, meeting these two at a club. This wasn't going to happen again fa' sho, but I was in the mood for a hard drink and some good company.

By the time we got to the club, the line was wrapped around the parking lot. Atlanta is always good for a good party. It seems like that's all them niggas do out there. A bouncer walked us to the front of the line and let us use the side entrance. Johnny was friends with the club owner. They played ball back in college.

The club was full of ballas. Not just men either. There were women wearing platinum jewelry with Fendi and Prada outfits. I'm not talking about that fake junk. These ladies had definitely been to Lennox Mall's finest shops.

Atlanta had some good-looking people. Every one dressed like they had money. We walked upstairs to the VIP section next to the bar. Johnny ordered a bottle of cham-pagne and we did tequila shots.

"Candice, you ready?" asked Toi.

"No, the question is, are you ready?"

After we got our buzz, we went to the dance floor.

"Hey girl, I know it's not a good time, but one of Johnny's teammates is meeting us here."

"Toi! Why you gotta do this now?"

"I'm sorry, but Johnny already made plans before you called. Besides, he may be what you need right now. I know you still horny from waiting for Fred for all that time. Hey, if he ain't all that, just let the nigga lick the cat."

"Well . . . we'll just have to see. Oh wait girl, my cell is buzzing. Here that nigga go again."

"Who?"

"Fred. Looks like I'ma have to get my number changed. He filled up my message center the last couple of days."

"Honey, do what you gotta do."

I turned off my phone for the rest of the night. I don't like playing games.

I noticed Johnny looking for his friend. Our table was adjacent to the entrance with a tall table between us. He spotted his friend, but his friend did not see him since the table was between them. Johnny got up and walked over to where his friend was standing.

Toi watched Johnny as he and his friend headed toward the bar to get more drinks before they joined us. I just kept talking to Toi. I really wasn't in the mood for another one of Johnny's friends.

Toi said, "Girl, he pointing over here. He is fine and looks just like yo type."

When I looked up, I damn near pee'd on myself. It was him. Not Fred, Mike. Oh my gosh, it's really him again.

What am I going to do? I know he saw me, so I can't disappear like the last time. And speaking of the last time I saw him in West Palm Beach, he had to be with Johnny because that's when Toi met Johnny. The world is really a small place.

I know Toi thought I was losing my mind. My eyes must've been opened pretty wide because she turned her top lip up and frowned as I took in the sight of that magnificent man. I could tear him up right now.

No . . . no Candice, calm down. I just need to breathe slowly and take things one step at a time. Okay, here we go.

My body got warm inside as I thought about that night. The smells, sounds, and tastes. It was like we were there again. I wanted to go over and say something, but I couldn't move.

Oh no . . . he was staring at me. I knew he recognized me, but wasn't sure from where. I read his lips as he asked Johnny, "Is that Toi's friend?"

Johnny shook his head yes, and they both looked at me.

They started walking toward the table. Toi and I stood up to walk over to the bar. As he came closer, I became more nervous. It was definitely him for sure. What would I say? What would I do?

"Michael, this is Toi's best friend," but before he could finish introducing us Michael said, "Candice?"

"Hi, Michael," I was so nervous, but I hoped that he didn't notice.

Toi and Johnny immediately started tripping.

"Candice, I did not know that you knew Michael."

Johnny looked at Michael as if he was about to say the same thing.

I whispered in Toi's ear, "That's the guy you and Amber never met that I went home with that night over a year ago."

"Damn, he's the one."

She looked away and started screaming with excitement. Y'all know how your girls do when they happy for you.

I guess it was all kind of strange because I did not have the Fred situation out of my system yet. For all I knew, Michael might turn out to be married, engaged, bisexual, or something. I was not trying to deal with more drama. With my luck, I knew he had to be twisted in one way or another. Anyway, I was not putting my faith in nobody but me for a good minute. And, y'all wonder why I put my money before my honey.

Michael just stared at me, not knowing exactly what to say. What could he say? I didn't know what I wanted him to say, if anything. This whole situation was driving me crazy.

He ended up saying, "I knew that was you back in West Palm Beach at that club. I was with Johnny that night, but you disappeared."

I can tell that he wanted something from me. I'm not trying to blow my own horn, but when this firecracker brings the heat, you will burn. In other words, he probably wanted some sex. You know though . . . I might be all wrong about Michael. He could be a decent man, but Fred left a real bad taste in my mouth. So, I'm moving slow with everything else in my life.

Michael grabbed my hands and said, "I can't believe that you have walked back into my life."

My hands were sweating.

"I didn't think I'd ever see you again." Before I could

respond, Mary J. Blige's "Missing You" came on, and he asked me to dance.

"Okay."

All right . . . I may be losing precious cool points by not taking full control of the moment. See, I may be a cold businesswoman, but I'm still a woman. Every now and then, a nigga can take your breath away. As just demonstrated oh so perfectly by Michael.

Michael and I didn't even notice Toi and Johnny were watching us. I don't think either of us even realized when they started dancing right next to us. I only saw him, and I think he saw only me.

And I wanted him to hold me.

All people need the feel of another human being every now and then. The warmth of a hand or the feel of a person's breath against your neck can make you feel alive. Yeah, there's nothing like the human touch.

I wanted to feel him close to me.

I often thought about that night we had together, even when I was wasting my time with Fred. In fact, I used to imagine that very night when I lay in bed next to Fred.

He held me close to him, and I laid my head on his chest as we danced. My body became numb. I began to smell his sweet body oil. The tighter he held me, the more my loins ached for his manhood. When I felt his cool breath against my neck, I barely kept my composure.

He kissed my neck softly and said, "You feel so good next to me."

I finally mustered up enough courage to ask, "Michael, do you remember that night? Do you remember how good it felt next to each other? Did you miss me or think about me at least once?"

I started rubbing my lips against his neck lightly, but I didn't kiss him. I wanted to tease him a little.

"Candice, you remember how good it felt when I was inside you?"

"Yes, yes I remember."

He continued with, "I still think about how sweet you tasted and how tight and warm it was."

Call me a freak, but it turns me on when a sexy man talks dirty to me. A lot of women like to front, but nasty words usually mean extra-nasty lovin'.

"Was it good to you? Candice, have you thought about me at all? Did you hope that you would see me again? I have wanted you since that night. Don't you want to see me again?"

The song went off before I got a chance to answer his questions. We walked off the dance floor hand in hand.

We went and sat at the table with Toi and Johnny. Michael ordered another bottle of champagne for us, while he drank Hennessey straight up. I drank just enough to keep my buzz going. I knew that I was giving him all this tonight, and I definitely wanted to be sober enough to enjoy every inch of him.

As we sipped our drinks, Michael asked me again if I wanted to see him. I guess he wanted to be sure that I was still actually interested in him.

"I'm not looking for a sexual relationship," I replied. I don't know what made me say that. I already told y'all that I wanted to ride him like a jackrabbit on Viagra. Nevertheless, I knew that I wanted more than that. After the drama that went down with Fred, I had to put my guard up extra tight.

In response to my seemingly crazy statement, he said, "I would like to get to know you. I want to know every little thing about you. After all, it's really the little things that end up counting the most. Now, if I stood here and pretended that being inside of you and tasting you wasn't on my mind, I would be lying, but I can wait."

If he only knew how much I wanted him, but I had to be strong. My first thought was just to screw him silly, but I didn't know what his plans were. If I had learned anything from the whole Fred ordeal, it's that taking things slow is not enough. You have to do a background check.

Y'all go ahead and laugh, but most people lie without a second thought. Like I've said time and time again, I'm getting too old for those unnecessary games we play. I need something real without all the drama. Anyway, I'll be damned if I let another nigga shake up my life, even a little. No . . . this time I'm not just going to pump the brakes, I'm bringing this thing to a complete stop. You know . . . to really assess the situation.

"Candice, can I have a number where I can get in touch with you? Before you go and disappear on me again."

I looked at him and for a fraction of a second all I saw was Fred. I guess that's why I said, "Are you married or living with anyone?"

"No. I've been waiting on you."

Yeah right Negro. I knew he was just running game, but I gave him my number anyway.

We sat there talking and holding hands, like we were old friends. We didn't get all deep or nothing, just good conversation.

Okay . . . Okay . . . most of the time I found myself staring at his lips, trying to catch a glimpse of that rabbit-fast tongue. Girl . . . I was almost in a trance when he finally said, "Are you ready to go?"

"Huh, yeah. I'd like that."

We said good-bye to Toi and Johnny. I know Toi wanted to say something; I could see it in her eyes. I didn't give her a chance to say nothing. I thought we should save all the talking for tomorrow. I had some booty business to take care of.

I thought Michael was going to ask me what hotel I was staying in, but he didn't. We just drove and talked.

I didn't ask him where he was going, and he didn't volunteer to tell. Truth be told, I didn't care as long as we ended up between the sheets.

I'm not trying to paint some fairy-tale romance with this, y'all. Right about then, the only thing I was thinking about was the good loving this man put on me after the last time I rode in a car with him.

We eventually arrived at a guard gate. I knew we had to be going to his house, but I still didn't ask any questions. Like I said, I had one thing on my mind.

His house looked like a mansion squeezed between the average-sized homes on either side of it. Inside, only one small light was on. Without a word, he took my hand and led me to the bedroom.

Oh but yes. Like Jigga said, "It's about to go down." And hopefully, he will too and it will be as good as the first time. You feel me?

I put down my purse, and when I turned around he was standing right behind me. He pulled me close to him and started kissing me. There's that sweet tongue I remembered.

"Michael . . ."

"Shhhh. Just relax."

He didn't let me say a word. He started kissing me on my neck, and then carried me to the bed. I know this sounds crazy, but I wish I could have videoed everything that Michael did to me, so when I needed this high again I didn't have to try and remember what he did and how he did it. I could just pop in the videotape, and see that good feeling he gave me, close my eyes and pretend he was holding me and he was inside me again.

The next morning we woke up to a woman standing in the bedroom door with a food tray.

"Oh Mr. Haynes? I'm so sorry. I didn't know you had a guest," stated the older black lady.

"It's okay Ida. Come on in."

She walked in carrying food on a tray.

"I made you breakfast."

I stuck out my hand and said, "Hi Ida, I'm Candice and you can set the tray right here."

I pointed to my lap. She set it down on my lap and then shook my hand. I was starving by this time. Michael really helped me build up an appetite.

"This looks so good. Is it for me?"

Ida smiled and said, "Sure Ms. Candice. I'll be right back with yours Mr. Haynes."

Michael lay there and held me while I stuffed food into both of our mouths.

"Eat, because I know you're hungry. We really worked up an appetite last night," I said.

Then, I leaned back and kissed his lips softly before continuing to feed him more eggs.

Ida brought the rest of the food, and we ate that too.

After we finished, I told him to turn over for a massage.

Rubbing his fine body made me horny, so I reached over and grabbed a condom off the nightstand. I rubbed his beautiful chocolate stick with my hand and put the condom on him. Then, I sat straight down on it while staring into his eyes. Mere words can't explain how good it felt to have him plunge deep inside me. I wanted him to see the pleasure he gave me.

After we both came, we sat in bed and watched movies. It felt so familiar, like we had been together before doing the same thing. In a sense, I guess we had.

When we got tired of watching movies, we took a bubble bath together in his Jacuzzi. I sat between his legs with my back against his chest.

When we got out, I put on a pair of his shorts, which were much too big on me, and one of his T-shirts that I tied in a knot in the back. His shorts hung on my hips, making my waist look smaller than it is.

The day was too beautiful to sit in the house, so I told him that I wanted to sit by the pool. I sat in the sun, while he sat next to me under a large umbrella. We listened to the radio and enjoyed the sun.

After sitting in silence for a while, we started talking about our lives. He told me what he wanted and expected in a relationship, and I told him what I wanted and expected.

"I want a man who understands me. Until he understands me and I understand him, we can't have a real relationship because we won't know each other fully. I want a man who won't give up on me or my love. When I decide to love someone, I love all of that person, good and bad. When things go wrong or get difficult, and they will get difficult, I will hang in there and I hope he would too. If we do get together, I would have to understand that you have a life like I do. But when we are around each other, it would be beautiful because I wouldn't ask you to give up your life for me, so don't ask me to give up mine for you. I would try not to ask for more than you can give. We would have to be honest with each other. I'm the kind of woman that needs to hear the truth, no matter if you think it would hurt me or not. I have to know that we are friends and we are able to communicate. I don't want to be the kind of woman that you can't be yourself around. I want to be able to go out with you and just hang. I can't even consider having a relationship with you if we can't be more than just lovers."

"Candice, I want you. I already know that I want you. I want to know that you are mine. The thought of you being with another man burns me up inside. I want this to grow into something special. Just like you, I don't want to get hurt. So, can we agree to try and be together starting now?"

"Let's spend some more time together first and see what happens. I want this to work too."

Now don't get me wrong, the thought of a one-on-one relationship frightened me, but what did I have to lose? I decided to try and give it all I had.

I stayed outside by the pool sitting in the sun tanning,

while Michael went inside to take a nap. He had to go to the field soon for a game later. They were playing at home and Toi was coming to get me when she dropped Johnny off at the stadium. That way, I could ride back with Michael.

After the game, we waited for them in the family lounge. Everyone already knew Toi was Johnny's girl, but they were wondering who I was with. They wanted to ask, but didn't. It's really something how the married women in the room were the main ones that looked insecure. They were probably hoping that I wasn't messing around with their man.

While we were waiting, Toi told me that Michael had a few girls, but she didn't think that it was nothing serious.

I knew that I had to be careful with this relationship because athletes have women throwing themselves at them all the time.

We followed Toi and Johnny to eat at a restaurant in Buckhead. While we were eating, Johnny's friend Toby came into the restaurant and walked over to the table.

"What's up playas? Good game."

Toby talked about the game and other stuff that was unimportant. He didn't look once at me or Toi. In fact, he didn't even acknowledge our presence.

Although I could've sworn I saw him cutting his eyes at Toi like a jealous woman.

Well, maybe it was just my imagination.

He talked for over fifteen minutes and continued to ignore us. Finally, when he stopped, Michael said, "Toby, this my baby Candice."

He finally decided to half look over at me and gave one of those fake smiles.

"Wat up?"

Then, he looked away and continued to talk with the guys. This let me know that he didn't want any small talk from me.

While the guys talked with Toby, I asked Toi, "Don't you know him? Isn't that the guy who is always at Johnny's house, his homeboy?"

"Yeah, he's the one who's always at the house."

Then she added, "He always refers to women as whores, bitches, gold diggas, or whatever degrading name he can think of."

I came to the conclusion that the brotha got issues, and I mean some serious issues.

Before Toby walked off he said, "Y'all still coming to meet us?"

Johnny looked at Michael.

"Are we still going?"

Michael looked confused.

"You go ahead. I have my baby with me, and I want to take her home."

"Why do I have to go home? Why can't I go with you?"

Then Johnny said, "My baby's going with me. She goes where I go."

I said while looking at Johnny, "Where ya'll going?"

Then, I turned to Michael and continued with, "Why can't we go?"

Michael looked and said, "They are going to Nicki's, a strip club."

"So! Why can't we go? I want to go too."

He looked at me with an expression of surprise and said, "Are you sure, baby?"

"Yeah. I'm sure. I want to go."

He didn't know that I had been to a strip club before. When you have mostly male friends all your life, you do a lot of things that most women don't. I went with Money and his boys because that was one of the very few places where he would relax. I knew I didn't want a woman, never tried it and wasn't interested in trying it. But, I enjoyed seeing the guys enjoy themselves. Anyway, I liked watching the dancers so I could learn some new moves for my man.

On the way to the strip club, Michael asked if I had ever been to one before.

I explained to him that I had been plenty of times because I have mostly male friends. I told him that I didn't have a problem with my man going to a strip club, as long as he didn't make it an everyday habit. There are some niggas that live in the strip club. Whenever you want to find them, all you have to do is go to the local shake joint. I can't deal with a man like that, or should I say I ain't trying to deal with a nigga who is a sex addict. Some freakiness on occasion is cool, but too much of the freaky-deaky is a real problem.

We met some other guys there and sat over in the corner. I could tell that Michael was very uncomfortable being there with me. Since this was my first time there with him, he didn't understand that I knew how to have a good time, no matter where I was.

Johnny and Toi were comfortable. They were talking and laughing, as they watched the girls dance on stage. He would give Toi the money, and she would go up and throw it to the dancer. One of the dancers did a split with her legs spread out sideways. While the booty cheeks sat on the stage floor, she moved one at a time up and down. I'd never seen anything like that before. The way Toi and Johnny were acting, I knew they had done this before.

I got up and told Toi to walk over on the other side with me. "Baby I'll be right back."

We went to find a fine girl to dance for Michael and Johnny. When we saw the one we wanted we told her to come over to the table where we were sitting.

The dancer came and stood in front of Michael. He looked scared, like he didn't want to do anything to upset me.

"She ordered this dance for you."

He started smiling, leaned back, and enjoyed the dance. When she turned around, I took his hand and slapped her behind with it softly.

Then I said, "Bend over, and let us see what you working with!"

Toi yelled, "Open it up! Open it up!"

She took her fingers and spread her cheeks apart. Damn, lil mama had her clit pierced with a big loop hanging from it. I know that had to hurt.

Michael was enjoying every minute of this. When he saw that I wasn't a jealous woman, he finally relaxed. He got a handful of ones and gave me some. We started throwing the money at the dancer. He called a dancer over to give me a dance. I leaned back and enjoyed it, but when she tried to touch me I said, "You can dance, but don't touch me."

She leaned up against me.

"You never had a woman before, huh?"

"No."

"You should let me be the first. I love high-yella women. You've never been eaten out good until you let a woman do it. A woman knows what makes another woman feel good. You should just let me go with you and your man tonight. I'll show y'all a good time."

"No honey. I'm strickly dickly, not interested."

"Let me know if you change your mind. My name is Champagne, but you can call me Lisa."

We sat there and got tore up. I got up and started dancing for Michael, and then I whispered in his ear, "I can't wait to get that good stuff tonight."

We left the club around 4:00 A.M. When we got into the car, I jumped over on top of Michael and said, "I want it now. I don't want to wait until I get home."

I pulled his hard pole out and put on a condom from my purse. I had already had my pants off, so I eased it inside of me.

"Give it to me Daddy."

When I said that, he started controlling my movements by bouncing me up and down on him. He gave it to me hard for around ten minutes, before he came. When I climbed off of him he said, "Baby, you are something else, but I love it."

I stayed in Atlanta for a week with Michael at his house. Surprisingly, we didn't have any woman problems. I expected to have a few since my staying with him was not planned.

Toi said that she was going to stay an extra day. Even though I didn't want to leave, I knew it was time for me to get back to the real world. Being with Michael felt like a fairy tale without an ending. I'm going to believe that it was meant to be that way.

TEN

Take time out and listen to the wise
Then you will be ready to handle the . . .

surprise, surprise

Hello! Candice! Please!"
Click!

I hung up the phone as soon as I heard Fred's voice. This was the fifth time he had called today. He was hitting me up back to back. Damn, it didn't matter if I kept hanging up on him. He was going to keep calling until I changed my mind. I had told him that I didn't want to see him anymore, but he acted like I hadn't said a thing. He still called every day, even though I hung up as soon as I heard his voice.

I'll never understand niggas. I once had a boyfriend in college that said "persistence overcomes any resistance." I guess most men follow this credo. However, I'm not a goofy immature adult anymore. So, fuck his persistence 'cause my resistance ain't moving.

Fred even left messages. In fact, y'all check this one out.

"Hey baby, please don't do this to me. I care about you. Baby, I need you."

I know . . . I know, but listen to this one.

"I'm coming to see you if I don't hear from you. We need to talk. We can't leave it like this."

There wasn't anything to leave, because I left before we could even get started. Men are so damn predictable though.

The next thing I knew, he'd be following me. He'd probably start sending me flowers and gifts. I'll never get why people think they can buy anything and everything. The one thing I'll never sell is my pride and dignity. I bet y'all thought I was gonna say my body. For the right price, heyyyy. Psyche!! For real though ladies, we have to set boundaries or men will just use and discard us like worthless trash. I can't talk for y'all, but I know I'm better than that.

Since Fred and I moved in the same circles, so to speak, it was only a matter of time before we ran into each other. It had already happened a couple of times, but I was always able to lose him in the crowds; that was the way it went until the last time our paths crossed. He grabbed my arm before I could walk away.

"Look Fred, I don't know what your problem is, but don't you have a diaper to change or Little League game to go to? I'm with someone else. You need to go home to your family."

"I don't care about nothing but you Candice. I know I hurt you, but just give me a chance. Let me make you happy. I love you, and I know you love me. So, I don't care about another nigga. All I care about is you baby."

Either he was smoking crack or his wife had knocked him into a point of retardation. He acted like I put my life on hold to cry myself to sleep, but it's not like that. I'm glad I got out before I started caring for him more than I did. Shoot, after all the no-good niggas I've been through I could endure anything, and I have. But you would think after three weeks he'd stop calling and get the hint, but he still calls every day.

I told him I was seeing someone, I didn't tell him who it was. I guess I should have, so that he'd know I wasn't playing. On the other hand, I was not trying to get Michael caught up in my drama. We still were trying to feel each other out anyway.

The season moved fast. Before I knew it, it was time for the All-Star game. But I refuse to duck and hide for the rest of my life. Who does this fool think I am? I've always thought that you should deal with problems head-on if avoiding the issue doesn't work.

I might run into Fred at the game. I was not looking forward to it, but this was my world too. It would be in Atlanta, and I couldn't wait to go. Michael said that I had to come and stay at his house. He made the team and said that his "Baby," who is me, had to be there with him.

Johnny and Fred made it also. Of course Toi would be there with her man, even though she hadn't talked much about going since she got back. It was going to be interesting to see Fred's reaction when he saw me with Michael. Maybe he'd get the message then.

I was really looking forward to seeing Michael. It had been almost two weeks since I last saw him. He flew down to see me on his day off because I had an important meeting and I couldn't get away. That made me feel good. It let me know that he respected my career and didn't expect me to just drop my responsibilities for him.

He was working with me on our relationship. Fellas did

y'all hear me. For those who weren't listening I'll repeat myself slowly. HE . . . WAS . . . WORKING . . . WITH . . . ME! You have to understand the word "with. " It means not trying to control the situation, but allowing for mutual control. If you really want to make a woman hot for you, do like Michael. I ain't even gon' lie, I wanted to bone his brains after he made such a selfless gesture.

Anyway, back to the Atlanta game.

Johnny made it as an alternate. The player that was picked before him was still hurt, so that opened up a space for him. To my surprise, Toi hadn't seen Johnny since she left three weeks ago. Usually, they wouldn't let a week go by without seeing each other. Toi had seemed disturbed by something ever since she came back. She told me she had something to talk about with me, but she didn't know how to yet. That caught me off guard because we talked about everything, and she has never hidden anything from me before.

We went to eat lunch several times, but she felt distant. I asked her what was wrong, but she said that she wasn't ready to talk yet. This whole talk, don't talk thing seemed like déjà vu. It was like Amber all over again. Man, I hope this girl ain't kill nobody. Nah, it can't be that serious because, like I told y'all, Toi don't got the stomach for real stressful stuff. Whatever the deal is, she'll talk when she's ready.

Toi called right before it was time for us to go to Atlanta. She needed to talk to me before we left because she wasn't sure if she was still going. Now I knew something was really wrong. Toi not wanting to see Johnny, unghh, unghh.

Something not right. So I suggested we go eat an early dinner. It'd give us enough time to get back home and pack for our trip.

Toi picked me up, and we rode to Boca Raton.

In the car, I asked Toi, "Hey girl, are you ready to talk?"

"Can we wait until we get to the restaurant? I need to think just a little more. I also want a couple of drinks before I tell you."

She made me promise that once she told me I would give her my honest opinion without judging her.

"You know me better than that Toi. After all these years, we have never done it any other way."

We were seated at a table right away and ordered drinks. I ordered red wine and Toi ordered a shot of Hennessey. After her second shot, and before we ordered anything to eat, she started to speak sadly and slowly. "Remember when you left me in Atlanta the last time you were there?"

Before I could answer, she said with tears in her eyes, "Well, I went to the airport the next day, but when I got there I noticed that I forgot my ticket at Johnny's house. I tried to call him so he could bring it, but he didn't answer the phone. I thought that he'd left early for the ballpark because that's the only time that I can't reach him. So, I jumped in a taxi and took it back to his house to get the ticket. He'd given me a key a while back, so I knew I could get in. I just knew that he was gone because he pulls his car in the driveway and not in the garage if he doesn't have much time. I opened the door and walked into the living room. I didn't see anybody. I went into the bedroom to get my ticket and when I went downstairs to get back into the taxi, I heard a funny noise. It was like something was bumping against something else in the bedroom by the back door. As I walked to the door, I saw Johnny and Toby."

She started crying harder and continued with, "I saw . . . I saw, uuh, uuuh . . ."

She couldn't get the words out, and when she tried to finish the sentence her face was covered with tears.

"I saw . . . Johnny, Johnny screwing Toby."

When she said this, she looked away from me, her eyes staring down to the floor. I was shocked, but I didn't respond for a few minutes. I tried to control the look on my face, but I was really taken for a loop.

Y'all know that I wanted to laugh. It was like a million jokes ran through my mind in a few seconds. I could hear a baseball announcer's voice saying things like, "He's coming home, folks," or, "Look at the way he handles that wood. That's why he's in the pros." I couldn't clown my girl like that . . . at least not yet anyway.

"Are you sure that is what you saw?"

"Yes, I'm sure! How could I mistake two big men hunching like dogs??!!!"

"What did you do? Did you go in? Did they see you?"

"No. I couldn't think straight. All I could do was leave."

Now I could understand why Toby hated women and why he despised Toi as much as he did. He wasn't Johnny's friend; they were booty buddies. It had to be going on since they were young because they were childhood friends.

That's one thing I always thought about football and baseball players. They wear all those tight clothes and love to touch on each other. They even shower together regularly. I was trying to not be too self-centered, but as soon as Toi told me this, I started to picture Michael at one of Johnny's fudge-packing parties. If Johnny likes boning men, who's to say that Michael ain't down too?

I felt empathy for Toi. The look on her face showed all her pain. She looked so confused and alone. Toi and Johnny were a perfect match; so I thought. They got along so well, and they couldn't stand to be away from each other. He had given her an engagement ring and asked her to marry him. She had said yes and they had planned the wedding for next summer.

What do you do when you think you have found the perfect match, a man that's respectable, acts like he can't live without you, treats you like his queen and shares everything with you, but then you find out there are more players involved in the game than you knew about?

What would you do? Walk away? Stay? The truth is . . . no one knows until it's them.

Just when life finally deals you the hand you been waiting on, something happens to let you know that it's not as good as you thought it was. Is there such a thing as a perfect, well not perfect but just a dependable relationship? Love can be so painful at times. Is it really worth the occasional joy it brings?

"Candice, what should I do? Should I leave him?"

Before I answered, I had to think carefully about what to say. Toi was in love with Johnny. He was the man of her dreams that she'd been waiting on. So, I tried to choose my words cautiously.

"Toi, I can't tell you what to do. You have to do what you feel in your heart."

"I don't know what I feel. This is all so crazy. I know I've done some freaky thangs, but why my man have to like what I like?"

"Well, do you love him? I mean, do you love him with all your heart and believe that he loves you despite what you saw?"

She didn't answer me. I know her mind had to be full of thoughts. God knows how I would have reacted to this situation.

She asked me again, "What would you do if you were me? Please, tell me! I'm lost . . . I don't know anything anymore."

"I won't lie to you. My first instinct would be to run. No matter how hard it would be for me, I'd probably just leave. But after I had some time, I'd just think about what's really important to me. If I could deal with knowing that my man is bisexual, then I might try. There're not many men out there that treat a woman like Johnny treats you. He adores you and lets you be you. He accepts everything about you; good, bad, freaky, or whatever. He just loves you and wants to be with you. This kind of love is hard to find, and if you are lucky to find it once, then you are truly blessed. One thing I have learned is that when you leave a man because of his ways, you only trade in one set of faults for another set. Child, no one is perfect. Since you know what you have already, you need to decide if you can deal with it for yourself."

Anyway, who am I to be giving anybody advice about relationships? My life when it comes to men hasn't been too much better than hers. The only difference is that I decide when and if I want to be bothered with a nigga or not.

She asked again, "But, would you leave him though?"

"I can't say. I know I wouldn't just roll over and act like nothing happened. Toi, I can't tell you what to do because I've never been that deep in love. However, I do know that AIDS is real, so you need to do something for your own sake."

"Will you help me if I stay? Will you help me come up with something to get Toby away from my man?"

"Yes, I will," I said as I assured her by touching her hand and leaning over to give her a hug. We ordered one more round of drinks and she thanked me for being her friend and always being there for her.

After we ate, we drove home with her making the decision to stay with Johnny and to go to the All-Star game as planned. Oh yeah, we also came up with a plot that is guaranteed to get Toby out of Johnny's life.

I realized that Toi was really in love. She had fallen hard, and I mean real hard. I don't know if I want to be in love like that. That's a scary kind of love; one I can do without. I have learned that in any relationship, you have to know the reason why you are there. Some get involved because of love, stability and/or financial security. But whatever the reason is, you have to have respect, commitment, trust, understanding, communication, and friendship. You have to be able to try and understand what is being communicated and trust that person enough to believe in what they are saying. This is an especially difficult thing to do when you've been cheated on once. Most people don't realize that a relationship can work without love, as long as you have the respect, commitment, understanding, trust, and friendship. It can last a lifetime without love, but one that has love only will not last, because love isn't always a sure thing. Love is way too unpredictable to depend on.

I'd rather trust in what I can control. The worst thing that can happen in this situation is that you waste a little time.

Toi and Johnny seemed to have a strong friendship along with their love. They respected each other, at least for the most part. Boning a nigga up the butt ain't exactly the most respectful thing to do when you have a woman. You know though . . . sometimes shit happens that throws salt in the game. But, is that enough to give up on something special?

Yeah, I can get deep at times too. I took a few Psychology and Philosophy classes back in undergrad. See, when you plan on going into a world filled with pimps, you have to learn how they think to avoid becoming just another hoe on the stroll.

Amber and Randy are a prime example of how love without nothing else can turn into disaster. Love is not strong enough to make a relationship last. I'm not talking about Agape, Storge, or Philia love, but Eros love. A love between a man and a woman that is physical and sexual. Peep game. Have you ever seen two homeless people in love pushing their basket, and sleeping under the bridge together? Hell no!! When things got tough somebody had to bounce and find a better way. Love didn't keep them together.

Deep down inside, I believed that Toi was making the right decision. Once you decide to love someone, you have to be able to deal with whatever comes up. When the heat gets too hot, you have to know when to get out. From where I was standing, I felt like their relationship was worth the fight.

When Toi dropped me off at home, she said she felt a lot better than when she came and got me.

I asked Toi if she wanted to come in for a drink, but she said no because she had to go home and pack too. Our flight was leaving at seven in the morning, so I didn't have much time to relax. I had to start packing right away. I hate rushing, but I was so exhausted from work and dinner that I had to take a few minutes to regroup.

I turned on my India Arie CD and went to my minibar for a glass of Merlot. There y'all go again, hating. No, I'm not boogie because I drink red wine. Everybody can't roll up a sweet and blow big to release stress. When you cross that invisible economic divide, as they say, shit gets real. In other words, I have way too much to lose to let what folks think make me do something stupid. Although I was tired, I was still hyped about seeing Michael. I could barely wait. Once I was relaxed and settled, I began to pack for the next day. Toi was picking me up at 5:45 in the morning, and I wanted to have everything packed and by the front door.

Just when I was closing up my last bag, I heard a knock at my front door.

"I bet that's Toi. She wanted a bottle of that champagne I got from overseas last year for our trip. She probably thinks I'ma forget it or something."

I opened the door without looking out the peephole.

"I had to see you Candice," Fred said and then pushed open the door.

"I can't talk to you right now Fred, I'm getting ready to leave town. What are you doing here?"

I did not trust myself alone with him. As soon as I opened the door I had flashbacks of how fine he was and the package that he had in his pants. I had always wanted to make love to him; I just never got the chance. I knew I had to keep my distance or he would be between my legs tasting this candy.

I knew he was going to start lying and begging. I wasn't in the mood for none of his Keith Sweat "baby please" bullshit. Why can't y'all niggas just go when it's over?

"Please Candice, just talk to me for a minute so I can explain what happened; so I can explain my situation."

What I couldn't understand was how he was gonna explain being married. Either you are or you aren't. I didn't want to hear anything he had to say, so I tried to get past him to open the door for him to leave. He stepped in front of me and said in an adamant tone, "I'm not leaving until you talk to me." He pulled me away from the door.

"I didn't make an extra trip here just to leave without talking to you."

My mind started racing . . . this nigga gotta be crazy. If I can just get to my dresser, I'ma bust a cap in his lying no-good stankin' butt for sho. Who did he think he was manhandling me like that? He done messed with the wrong one today.

Then he said softly, "Please Candice, please just give me a minute of your time. Don't I deserve that?"

"You don't deserve nothin' from me. I was honest with you from the very beginning and you lied. Well, I can't say you lied, but you chose not to tell me that you were married."

Since this nigga wasn't planning on leaving no time soon, I walked into the bedroom to finish packing my last bag. He followed me, still trying to explain something that I didn't want to hear.

"Baby, I know I should've told you that I was married, but I didn't want to lose you. I've been married for nine years. It was something that happened right out of high school. I feel like I owe her. I can't leave her, but I'm not in love with her. Please, I need you."

He tried to put his arms around me, but I pushed him away and moved to the other side of the room.

"Get out of my damn house, Fred! Please leave me alone! We really don't have anything else to talk about."

I started walking toward the front door, but he grabbed me and held me with a tight grip. With his other hand, he grasped my head and forced me to look at him.

"Candice, I love you. Baby, I love you. You make me happy. I don't know how I fell in love with you when I've never made love to you, but I did. I want you. I need you. Baby, please, please don't do this to me."

Now what this fool really needed was some good psychiatric help or a hearing aid. He just wasn't trying to feel a word I was saying.

He tightened his hold on me and pulled me closer to him, as he held my face between his hands and started kissing me as though he was on fire.

As I struggled to get away, we fell on the bed. I tried to get my head loose from between his hands, wriggling my body so I could get from under him.

"No Fred! Please stop, don't do this!"

I yelled louder, "Stop Fred! Stop!"

My voice weakened. I felt like I was going to cry, but nothing came out.

"I can't stop. I want you. I need you."

He started rubbing his hands up and down my body while breathing heavy.

"Baby relax and let me make you feel good. Give me all of you. Let me give you what you need."

"Stop Fred! Please stop!"

I knew what he wanted, and I knew that he wasn't going to stop until he got it. I started moving my body quickly from side to side, but his body's weight wouldn't let me get free.

God, I couldn't believe this was happening to me. I've always been so careful. Why? Why me?

He started kissing me around my neck and opened up my robe to try and suck my nipples. He was breathing real loud by this time, saying that he couldn't help it because he needed me. He had unlimited access to my entire body. I didn't have anything on under my robe.

He was rubbing his hands everywhere, touching me between my legs trying to pry them open. I kept them tightly closed. He cupped my breast in his hand and started licking my nipples very softly from one to the other while still holding me down with the weight of his body.

My head started spinning. This can't be real. This has to be a dream. I refuse to believe this is happening to me.

"Please stop! Don't do this Fred! Please get off me! Stop! I'm seeing someone. I have somebody now. Please leave me alone!"

I kept trying to get away from him, but he held me down harder. He ignored everything I said and continued to rub and kiss my body. He vigorously put his hand between my legs and stuck his finger inside me and then took it out and put it in his mouth.

"Oh, you taste so good. Let me taste you baby. Let me make you feel good."

He forced his finger inside me again and started pushing it in and out. I wanted him to stop. I begged for him to stop, but he wouldn't.

He continued to kiss me on my stomach and lick his way down to my pubic hairs. He kissed the top of my clit, barely touching it with his tongue. My head was still spinning, but this was a little different. My sugar walls started pulsating faster with each touch of his tongue. Each kiss was so perfect and concise as he moved up and down from my stomach to my breast and down, trying to get to my clit. It started feeling good, but I didn't want to like it. I didn't want to enjoy what he was doing, but his soft lips and wet tongue just kept licking and kissing. And my whole body felt like it was spinning.

I didn't want him to think that I was enjoying what he was doing, so I yelled . . . a little weaker.

"No Fred stop! Please stop! Don't do this!"

As he kept me pinned down, he whispered in my ear, "I want you baby. Please let me satisfy you. Let me give it all to ya! I promise you'll like it. I can't stop; I've been waiting on this moment for too long."

He pried my legs open and started kissing my inner thighs, using his shoulders as a wedge. He lifted my butt off the bed and pulled me up to his face. He kissed my clit gently and then went back to my inner thighs and sucked them softly. By this time, I was whispering my rejection.

"Fred please stop! Don't!"

I pleaded with him, "Please let me go."

With every lick, I got weaker. As he licked my clit softly, the only thing I thought about was how good his warm wet tongue felt.

As he kept kissing, the voice that was yelling and whispering and pleading for him to stop turned to moans of pleasure.

"Oh Fred stop. Oh Fred, don't. Oh! Oh Fred! Fred! Oh yeah! Oh yeah! Yes! Yes!"

At that moment, the only thing I could do was surrender to his passion. My body went limp and I lay there waiting for each kiss, wanting more, wanting all of him.

"That's my baby. Let me take care of you. Yeah, that's my baby, relax and let Daddy satisfy you."

He looked into my eyes as he outlined my face gently with his hands. He breathed softly in my ear as he licked my earlobe. He continued to breathe softly while he hungrily kissed me around my neck, ears, and shoulders. His breath on my skin kept my nipples hard and at attention. He put his tongue in my mouth so that I could taste him. He was delicious. The aggressive man that entered my home had turned into an unselfish, gentle, and passionate lover. He held my hands as he kissed me and touched me all over. He rubbed his beautiful body against mine, as he moved up and down on me.

"Candice, I want you to enjoy this. I want you to want me like I want you. Tell me to stop if you don't want me to go any further. Tell me to leave."

I lay there enjoying his touch, his kiss, his smell, and his gentleness. I wanted him. I couldn't bring myself to tell him to leave, even though I knew that it was wrong.

I guess the feelings I had for him never truly left. I thought I was over him, but I had just pushed my desires deep down inside of me.

"I want you Fred. I want all of you now. Please don't stop."

He opened up my candy lips and slowly flicked his tongue. Just when my juices were about to erupt, he stopped and said, "I don't want you to come yet."

He had only been kissing it for a short period of time before I started to climax. I was so hot and horny. The thought of him inside me made my juices flow nonstop. He turned me over on my stomach and licked his tongue up and down my back. My faucet wouldn't stop. I was flowing like a broken water line. I was so hot and it felt like I was going to burst. He stuck his tongue in my butt as he moved his finger slowly in and out of me.

My body jumped as if I was having convulsions. I had surrendered totally and completely. I lay there enjoying the wonderful sensations that he was giving me. Each time he licked or touched my body, it jumped with excitement and eagerness.

Then he came up slowly and looked me in my eyes. "Tell me you want it."

I looked down at his goods. I had forgotten just how big it was. Damn. I couldn't keep my eyes off it. As he rubbed his fat ten inches in his hand, I didn't hesitate to tell him what I wanted.

"Give it to me Fred. I want it."

"Are you sure? Are you sure this is what you want?"

I didn't say a word. I just pulled him to me and kissed him

with all the passion I had inside. He held me tightly, reached between my legs and pushed his D inside me.

"Oh baby, you feel so damn good! It's so tight it won't let all of me in." He kept pushing it in me gently.

"Fred, wait! Let me get a condom."

I tried to get up, but he held me down and said, "No I want to feel all of you."

I begged him to let me get the condom, but he kept moving his thick pole around; trying to force all of it inside me. I looked up at him with tears in my eyes, only then did he relent.

I got a condom and the KY Jelly, and put it on him. He laid me down and entered me.

My walls gripped every part of his thick pole as he moved slowly inside of me. The sensation he gave me as he moved in and out of me made me want to open up completely to him. I wrapped my legs around his back and squeezed him closer and further into me.

As he tender dicked me, he asked, "You mine, ain't you mine? I love you Candice. I love you."

He looked in my eyes and said, "This mine, Candice. Tell me this mine."

I didn't say anything, so he slowed down the strokes and said again, "Tell me you love me Candice. Tell me this is mine."

I didn't want him to stop. I had to have him inside me, so without thinking, I said, "Fred, I love you. This yo pussy."

As he made love, he adamantly said, "Nobody gonna get daddy candy."

"I!" followed by a gentle stroke, "Don't!" a slightly harder thrust, "Want!" a harder poke, "Nobody!" an even harder plunge, "In daddy's pussy!" a series of forceful steady full-length pumps.

"It's yours! It's yours!" I screamed with pleasure. Then I yelled each time he moved that big black lacquered pole in and out of me. I dug my nails into his shoulders and pulled him closer.

"Give it to me! Oh it's good! Oh it's good baby, please don't stop! Don't stop! Please! Don't stop! Please! Please!" I begged him to give it all to me, and he did. We both came at the same time and laid there panting for air.

I sat there for a few minutes trying to compose myself, realizing what I had just done. I couldn't believe I just screwed the hell out of Fred. What was I thinking? What was I gonna do?

He moved over to my side and held me tightly. He held me like he thought I was going to sneak away and leave.

I tried to get up so I could get a wet washcloth to wipe us off, but he held me firmly and wouldn't let me move. I dozed off thinking about the mistake I had just made.

I dreamed that Michael had walked in while I was sucking Fred's D, and he shot both of us. I could tell right now, nothing good was gonna come from this.

I didn't hear Toi knocking on the door. When I didn't answer, she let herself in. She walked into the room and was surprised when she saw us naked in the bed together.

"Candice," she said softly and touched me on my shoulder.

When I opened my eyes, I knew that she was shocked. She stood there for a moment just staring with a smirk on her face. I can only imagine what she was thinking. Last night, I talked about how wonderful Michael was and how I really wanted our relationship to work; and this morning, I'm in bed naked with a man who I claimed I didn't want to see again with the sweet smell of sex lingering in the air.

Now, Toi is not the type to judge, because she knows that sometimes shit happens. I knew that she was wondering how all of this took place in such a short period of time without her even knowing that it was going to go down. Hell, I didn't know how it really happened. All I knew was that I enjoyed it. I mean I really enjoyed it. I knew I had made a big mistake, but what's done was done and there was nothing I could do about it.

The only thing that I regretted was the fact that I liked it all so much. Maybe because the passion had built up after we spent so much time together, or because he was so gentle, or because of the way he held me and looked at me while he was inside me. Just the thought made my body shiver. What was I going to do? He was a married man, and I did have a man now, or at least I had one before last night. I knew that I shouldn't see him again. I kept telling myself that I wouldn't, but I knew that I was lying.

Can a woman want two men or love two men at one time? Now I understand what a man means when he's messing around knowing that it's wrong, but he just can't let the other woman go. I was so confused, but I did know right from wrong. I knew that no one could come before Michael because we had something special that I must consider, and I was not going to let him go.

I got up out of the bed and told Toi to follow me into the

bathroom. Before we could get in there good, she said in a low scream, "Now girl, you just had to get some of that good stuff! I know it was good because Amber told me how good and big he was. I don't know. He looks DAMN good lying in that bed naked. I don't know . . . are you . . . are you . . . are you sharing?"

When Toi asked me that question I wasn't surprised. She knew who was off limits and who wasn't. She would never ask me that about Michael, nor I about Johnny. The ones we cared about were off limits, that was the rule. On the other hand, everybody else was there to be had. All she had just gone through with Johnny, I knew she needed something to take her mind off of it, if only for a few minutes.

I didn't hesitate to tell her to go ahead and get it. I wanted to see him screw her. I wanted to be mad at him. I knew he'd make love to her just as passionately as he had to me and that would let me know that I didn't mean a thang to him. Sometimes we all have to do stupid things to get our lives back in perspective.

Toi took all her clothes off and went over to Fred. He was still asleep when she took his D in her hand, put it in her mouth and swallowed half of it. As he began to gain consciousness, he was startled at the fact that it wasn't me. I told him it was cool, and he didn't seem to have any problem with it either.

After he was as hard as steel, he put a condom on and began to stuff all his meat inside her. He didn't moan or even look her in the eyes. He wasn't gentle or nothing. It was different with me.

I was wrong. I was really wrong. He gave it to her with the

same force as he did Amber; without feeling, without passion. It was just straight fucking. Damn him.

We had to run through the airport, rush through security and hope that the airplane door wouldn't close before we got there. As we ran to the gate, I started thinking about how much I missed Michael. I really needed to see him to take my mind off of all the madness that went on last night.

Part of me wished that we missed our flight. It would give me more time to digest everything. I know I'm trippin'. I have feelings for a married man who I saw bone my two best friends. On top of all that, I'm falling for a man who thinks I've been totally monogamous.

We barely made our plane. Toi sat on the plane talking about how good Fred's D was. I regretted going to bed with him last night, but it happened. I just needed to try and forget about it. Michael meant everything to me, and I didn't want to lose him.

I already thought about what y'all thinking. I shoulda took that into consideration before we had sex. I have to put what happened behind me though.

As the plane landed, Toi got a little apprehensive about seeing Johnny. She knew she had to pretend that nothing had happened. But, how can you pretend that you don't know your man is screwing his supposed best friend in the behind? She had to have a lot of strength to even deal with him let alone try to work it out. I prayed that this week would be good to her and our plan would work out like we hoped.

"Hey baby."

I ran into Michael's arms and held him tightly. With him I

felt safe and secure. I didn't want to let that feeling go. He held me as if he needed to hold me as much as I needed to hold him. He smelled so good. I ran my hands up and down his arms, looking into his eyes as he told me how much he missed me. I knew this was where I belonged, and I would not be stupid and lose it for anything or anyone. Yeah, at that moment, I knew that I definitely would not be fooling around with Fred anymore. That big thang, no matter how good it was, wasn't worth giving up the sense of security I felt with Michael.

ELEVEN

Rent needs to be paid
The bills and car note are due,
Baby need milk, food,
clothes, and shoes too;
A single mother won't think twice
She definitely has the clue,
That a woman gotta do what . . .

a woman gotta do

Michael and I waited with Toi for Johnny. I could tell by how quiet Toi was that she wasn't looking forward to seeing Johnny this soon. When he finally showed up, Toby was in the car with him. Damn, here we go again. I looked at Toi and saw the hesitation in her eyes. I imagine that seeing those two together brought back that horrible picture to her mind. I walked over to her and said, "Sister girl, you have to be strong. Are you sure that you want to go through with it?"

She looked at me for a minute.

"Yes I do."

"Well, you have to stick to the plan and put on your best performance. We'll soon have Toby out of his life, but you have to be patient."

Before she could respond, Johnny jumped out of the car and was already picking her up, turning her around and kissing her. He told her how much he missed her and that she couldn't stay away from him that long again. He was so excited to see her. It was hard for me to imagine him with anybody but Toi, especially a man. But, you never know. From experience, the most manly of men are usually the ones with a tank full of sugar.

I watched her to see if she could handle it. She could. She held him and kissed him back. I looked over at Toby in the car just to see his reaction. He had the same stupid look on his face that he had the last time I saw him. He had to go. He hated to see them together, but he knew that there was nothing that he could do about it. As I watched Toi and Johnny, I could see that he genuinely loved her. He just had a secret passion; the booty.

Michael gave Johnny a pound and told him not to expect to see us later. He wasn't sharing me with anyone tonight. My baby wanted me all to himself. I gave Toi a hug and waved bye as we walked away.

A stretched white Navigator limousine pulled up in front of us. The driver got out and opened the door. I looked around for the person that the driver was picking up. Michael said, "Baby, your chariot awaits."

I didn't know that he'd rented a limousine to pick me up. My man was full of surprises. I was eager to know what was next on his agenda, but I didn't ask any questions. I just got in, snuggled against my baby, and enjoyed the ride.

It was a hot, humid, and muggy summer day in Atlanta, but it was still beautiful. Michael knew that I like sunlight, so he pulled back the cover of the sunroof. He turned on a Keith Sweat disc and made me a mimosa.

I remember telling him before that my favorite CD was the first one Keith Sweat released. When he put on that track, I felt all my concerns melt away.

"Relax baby. Let me take off your sandals," Michael said.

He massaged my feet with peppermint massage oil. Just as I started to relax, I felt his tongue licking up my leg.

"Oh baby, what you doing? Oh yeah . . . you know exactly what Mama likes."

He kissed and licked me softly, until I came. He used a towel to wipe the wetness from between my legs.

I've never met a man like Michael. He aims to please and will do whatever it takes to satisfy. Most men with money are very selfish and couldn't please a woman if their life depended on it. I knew Michael hadn't treated all his women as good as he treats me and that was what made our relationship special. My feelings for him were strong. For the first time in a while, I knew that I meant something to a man, my man. Although I believe in that whole "I'm a woman, hear me roar" stuff about loving yourself first, it's always good to know that your man is down for you too.

"Come on sugar, let mama get some," I purred as he held me.

"I just wanted to satisfy you and taste your sweetness. You've been gone away from me for too long, and I just couldn't look at your beauty and not taste you. We'll finish the rest later. Right now, I want you to let me hold you until we get to where we're going." He wrapped his arms around me, and I melted.

I know I'm no angel, but this was as close to heaven as I'll probably get. If I could just have put my life on pause at that moment, I'd say that I'd found my little slice of perfection.

The limo kept driving, and I obediently followed Michael's orders. I kept my eyes closed and inhaled as much of his scent as I could.

Our first stop was an exclusive hotel in Buckhead for their champagne brunch. It was a forty-minute wait, but since the hostess knew Michael played ball, we got seated right away. I went straight to the omelet bar and got an omelet with turkey, cheese, tomato, and green peppers. The breakfast sausage smelled good, but I had to pass on it.

You know, I try to stay away from the beef and pork. Actually, I eat very little beef and no pork at all. It helps me to keep my hourglass figure at exactly an hour. Don't get me wrong, I'm no health freak. Yo girl still cooks with pork to season food. Hell, when you grow up on the stuff, it's hard to let it go completely.

Michael went to the seafood bar and piled up on the shrimp and lobster cocktails. As I watched him walk back to the table, I thought about how much it would hurt to lose him. I thought about the mistake I made with Fred. Look, I know I was wrong, but do you have to keep judging me? Yeah, I'm talking to you reading this book. Whatever comes my way, I know I brought it on myself. Out of all of the dumb mess I could've done, why did I have to go and screw Fred? I knew that I couldn't take that chance again. I actually think that I love Michael. At least, I know I love the person that he is and the way he treats me. Isn't that enough? *Don't even think about trying to answer that.*

After we ate, we went across the street to Phipps Plaza, a popular shopping center for the wealthier residents of Atlanta. Michael had already picked out two outfits that he wanted me to try on.

"I went shopping earlier, and I knew these outfits would look good on you. I asked the salesperson to hold them until you came back with me. I hope you don't mind."

"No baby, that's so sweet."

First, I tried on a lavender sundress. It had wide spaghetti straps and the neckline was cut low in the front. It showed off my perfectly round size 36Ds, if I must say so myself. It fit tight around the waist and hung loose around my hips. The dress was made of rayon and silk. It was very elegant, the kind of sundress that can be worn on the beach or to dinner.

The second outfit was a silk turquoise ensemble. The sarong skirt fit like a loose mermaid skirt. It started just below my waist and stretched just past my knees. The top fit snug, but not too tight, against my body. This outfit was definitely saying something. It was sexy and chic. I walked out of the dressing room, giving my best "working it" walk. The sight of Michael standing there in awe made me work it even harder.

"Baby, that's gorgeous. You have to wear it to the players' party."

I kissed him on the lips and said, "I love them both. Thank you."

Michael had good taste and made sure his woman was looking good too. I couldn't wait to wear my outfit. I wanted to make him proud.

When we left the mall, we went to the day spa down the street. Michael had our massages set up so both of us could be in the same room. Also, I got a facial and a body wrap. I never knew that going to the spa with my man could be so romantic. After he finished his massage, he had to go to the stadium. I stayed and finished my day of pampering.

When I left the spa, I met Toi for a drink at a sidewalk café. Michael and Johnny were at the field, so we took time to discuss what we had to do to make sure Toby was out of the picture for good. We decided to meet when the guys went to the park.

TWELVE

Life, love, disappointment, happiness,
loathing, distress, peace, loyalty,
jealousy, commitment, betrayal,
hate, envy, and sin.
It's all bound to happen so . . .

let the games begin

Toi wasn't her usual talkative self. She became quiet and very nervous as we approached Johnny's house. Her voice trembled when she spoke, and she was shaking like a dried-up leaf on a tree. It was obvious that she was apprehensive about seeing Toby. However, I knew she realized that this situation must be addressed soon.

"Are you sure this is the best time to do this? Should we really go through with it, Candice?"

"Look Toi, the question is, are you sure that you want to do this? Do you want Toby to be part of y'all's life forever? If you don't mind sharing yo man . . . hey, it's up to you. I can't make the decision for you. You have to decide what direction you want your relationship with Johnny to go, not me. So I'ma ask you one more time, are you sure you want to do this?"

"Yeah, I want him out of our lives, but you don't have to put it like that!"

"You must've forgotten what you're dealing with, and what brought us to this point in the first place. If you want things to change, then you gotta do this. Now is the best time. This definitely ain't the time for reservations, Johnny will be home soon, and we need to be finished before he gets here."

When we pulled into the driveway, we saw Toby's car. As expected, Johnny's Porsche wasn't in the garage. He should be back in about fifteen minutes, so we had to get started immediately.

We walked into the house and saw Toby sitting in the den playing video games. We knew that he wouldn't speak to us but we spoke to him anyway.

"What's up Toby?" He ignored us and continued to play the game as if we hadn't said a word.

We walked past him and continued down the hallway that connected the master bedroom to the rest of the house. Suddenly, Toi stopped and turned around facing the den. She hesitated for a brief moment, took a deep breath and headed toward the den where Toby was sitting.

"Why is it that every time I come to town, you act like you have an attitude problem when you see me?"

Toby ignored her and continued to play the video game. If we hadn't known better, we'd probably have thought he didn't hear a word she said. He didn't acknowledge her presence at all, not even by a blink of the eye.

Then Toi said in a harsher tone, "Why the hell do you act like you're jealous of me and Johnny's relationship? You know what, you act like a jealous girlfriend."

Toby looked up at her with his eyes so wide that they looked like they were about to pop out of his head.

"Hoe, me and Johnny go way back. You don't have nothing with him that I don't have, and if you don't know it or not . . . you ain't all that!"

Then he rolled his eyes, snapped his neck, and turned his head away from her like he was a punk queen or the way an upset hood rat would do when she's arguing with her boyfriend.

By this time, Toi was fuming.

"You ain't nothing but a homeboy that don't wanna work and will do anythang for a free ride, probably even suck a thang or two, huh nut breath?"

Toby jumped up, huffing and puffing, with his fists tightly closed. You could tell that he was trying to refrain from knocking the hell out of her. He got in her face and said, "You ain't running a damn thang around here. If you only knew what you had, then you'd shut yo damn mouth and not talk so damn much, you . . ."

Toi cut him off before he could finish, "What do I have? Tell me nigga! What do I have you punk?!"

I saw Johnny's car coming down the street and I gave Toi the signal. Toi continued with, "What do I have? You want him, don't you? You want my good dick. You punk. You want Johnny to give ya what's mine, don't you?"

By this time, Toby was so mad that his face had swollen and he started yellin' and calling Toi all kinds of names. I signaled again for Toi to hurry. I wanted her to know that Johnny was at the gate. She needed to hurry up and come over to where I was standing.

She walked over to me and said, "Go ahead do it now!"

Before she could finish, I reached back and punched her

with all the strength I had in her eye and nose. She acted like she ain't feel no pain. When she saw Johnny's car, she just ran out of the house holding her face screaming and crying. Her eye had swollen and her nose was bleeding.

Johnny saw her, stopped the car abruptly, and then jumped out.

"Baby what's wrong? Who did this to you?"

The taxi I had called pulled up before Toi could answer him.

"Come on Toi, let's go. Let's get out of here."

"Wait a minute! What's wrong with her? Who did this?" Johnny yelled as he demanded an answer.

Toi sat on the ground, just crying and screaming, trying to talk as snot and blood ran out of her nose. She tried to explain, but he couldn't understand anything she was trying to say. Her nose was bleeding profusely, and her eye had turned blue.

She started speaking slowly, but still sounding confused, "Toby said . . . Toby said . . . I asked Toby why he did not like me because he never speaks to me . . ." she sniffed snot back up her nose as she tried to talk, "and he just went off on me. He said I wasn't getting nothing from you that he wasn't getting. He said he was getting the . . . he was getting the dick too." Toi was crying uncontrollably at this time.

She looked up into Johnny's eyes and said, "I told him he was a damn liar. Then he punched me in my eye . . ."

"He said what?" Johnny yelled. He was so mad that sweat started rolling down his face, and his eyes became blood-shot red.

Toi continued to cry and yell. "I told him he was lying.

Look what he did to my face. I can't go back in there. I won't go back in there. He hates me, and he hates seeing us together. I gotta go. I'm sorry, but I gotta go. "

I pulled her by the arm and told her to come on and get in the taxi. Johnny was begging her to stay. He said he'd take care of everything, but she got in the taxi anyway.

"Johnny, that was some sick stuff yo boy said and did to her. I won't let Toi go back in there with that crazy fool. I'll take her to Michael's house with me. She'll be fine. I'll call you later and let you know how she's doing."

As I closed the door, Johnny was still begging for Toi to stay. I put Toi's head against my chest and held her.

"It will be all right," I said to her as the taxi drove away and left Johnny standing in his driveway.

When we got down the street, I whispered in Toi's ear, "Damn girl, you need to be an actress. You trifling little heifer you." When I said that, she almost burst out laughing.

"You didn't have to sucker punch me that hard. I didn't know you was going to hit me like I was a nigga," she said softly.

I laughed aloud and stared at the taxi driver to let her know that we had to continue this conversation when we were alone.

When we got to Michael's house, I led Toi to the guest bedroom and gave her a bag of ice to put on her eye. I hoped her makeup would cover up whatever bruise was left in two days. We'd be attending the players' party then.

I wanted to get her in bed and settled before Michael got home. If he saw her face today, he'd ask too many questions. He'd be worried because he always says he can't stand a nigga that hits on a woman.

"Hey baby," Michael said as he walked into the kitchen and gave me a hug and kiss.

"Oh that feels good, I really need that right now." I stood there in his arms enjoying his touch and sweet smell. Just when he started kissing me around my neck, the microwave buzzer went off.

"Oh wait, the soup is ready," I said.

"Are you eating soup for dinner?"

"No, this is for Toi. She's in the guest bedroom. She and Toby got in an argument, and he punched her in the eye. She left Johnny's house and came over here," I explained as I took the soup out of the microwave.

"He did what? That nigga did what? Where was Johnny when he did that? What did Johnny do?" he asked with concern.

"Johnny was coming up when we were leaving. I don't know what he said to Toby because by that time we'd already left the house."

Michael walked to the guest bedroom with me to take Toi the soup. He was pissed when he saw Toi's eye. He picked up the telephone and called Johnny, but he didn't get an answer. Just as he hung the telephone up, the doorbell rang. It was Johnny. We knew he'd come over, but we didn't expect him so soon. Both Toi and I were surprised when we heard his voice over the intercom.

When Michael walked out of the room to go and unlock the front door, Toi looked puzzled and said, "Candice, do you think he's mad at me? Why do you think he came so soon?"

Toi looked worried, as if Johnny knew what we'd done.

Before I could answer, Johnny walked into the room and just stared at her. She was lying with her back to him. She didn't look up when he said her name. He sat next to her on the bed and started rubbing his fingers through her hair.

"Baby, I'm so sorry. I'm so sorry this happened to you, but I've taken care of everything. He won't be hurting you again," he said softly as he rubbed his hand through her hair.

At that moment, I knew that everything would be fine. So Michael and I walked out of the room to give them some privacy.

We went into the den and played cards as we listened to music. Twenty-five minutes later, Johnny and Toi walked out hand in hand.

Johnny looked at Michael and said, "Man, I'm taking my woman home so I can take care of her."

I got up, hugged Toi, and told her to take it easy for the rest of the evening. I asked Johnny to call me tomorrow before he went to the field to let me know if Toi felt like going to the mall to shop for her outfit for the party. I looked at Toi with a "you go girl" expression on my face as they walked out of the door. He asked me to come in the morning and keep her company when he and Michael went to the field.

When I went over to Johnny's house the next day, Toi filled me in. Johnny made Toby leave. He didn't let Toby say or explain anything. He told Toby that he loved Toi and couldn't let anyone come between them. I didn't think that Toby knew anything about Toi's eye, because Johnny didn't go into detail with him and Toby didn't see me punch her. Johnny just made it clear that Toi came first in his life and that she was going to be his wife. Johnny told Toby to leave his house forever.

Well, our plan worked. Now, let's just hope Toby stays out of their lives for good.

THIRTEEN

You cheated and hurt me
That was not in the plan,
What must I do
To find an honest man?
I'll let you go and
Do all that I can,
To forget about the lovin'
Because I finally understand,
That the disrespect is why . . .

I ain't your woman

The next afternoon, Toi and I went to the mall to find Toi some shoes for her party outfit. I got back to the house around seven. I thought that I'd find Michael sleeping, but he wasn't. He was sitting on the chaise longue in the bedroom, waiting for me. There were two glasses of Merlot on the end table next to him.

"Come here baby," he said. His sexy voice sent chills up my spine.

He patted the seat next to him. When I sat down, he handed me one of the glasses of wine.

We sat in silence for a few minutes, then he stood up and pulled me up next to him. He gently pulled the straps of my sundress off my shoulders and let the dress fall to the floor. He watched me with those alluring passionate eyes as I stood there wearing only a red G-string. He kissed my nipples softly, and led me into the bathroom.

The dim candlelight made it almost impossible to see in the room. Scented candles were neatly arranged on the countertops and around the Jacuzzi. The Jacuzzi was full of bubbles and what looked like a zillion exotically colored roses sat on the countertop adjacent to the tub. Everything was so beautiful. I looked at Michael and was about to tell him how beautiful everything was, but he put his lips to mine and said, "Don't speak, just enjoy the moment."

He slipped off my G-string and told me to get into the water.

I slid into the luscious water and rested my neck on the bath pillow. I closed my eyes and let the bubbles rise up to my shoulders.

"Baby, is the water okay?" he asked.

"It's perfect. Just like you."

Then he handed me my glass of wine and the card that came with the roses. The card read, "Just because I love you, Michael."

I looked at him with tears in my eyes. He said, "Do not say anything, just close your eyes." When I closed my eyes, he massaged my shoulders as I enjoyed K-Ci & Jojo's CD. The music played softly through the wall speakers, the candles' sweet odors gently wafted through the air, and his touch soothed me. I relaxed to truly savor the moment. I knew now for sure that I was blessed to have Michael as a part of my life.

After I got out of the water, he wrapped a towel around

me and carried me to the bed. He lovingly massaged oil over my entire body. When he finished, he said, "I'm going to take a shower, wait right here and do not move. Is there anything you want before I get into the shower?"

I pulled him on top of me and said, "Yes, I want you now."

He started kissing my body, but I rolled over on top of him and said, "I have a taste for you right now." Before he could respond, I grabbed his perfect protruding chocolate stick and sucked him as he softly moaned. I savored him until he exploded into my mouth.

"Now baby, you can go take your shower."

We both had to get ready for the party. I was so relaxed that I thought about just going to bed, but it was my baby's big night. I had to be there.

Michael put on a tailor-made suit that fit him perfectly. His tie was the same color as the dress that he bought for me to wear to the party. He sported some black ostrich shoes and a three-carat diamond stud in each ear. He looked good, and I was proud that he was my man.

"You're looking so beautiful and sexy. I better keep you close to me because I want everyone to know that you are my woman," Michael said, as he guided me to the car.

Toi and Johnny met us at the party. She was looking like a star in the fuchsia dress we had picked out at the mall. Her skirt was long with a split in the center. It showed off her bowlegs that seemed to drive men crazy. The top of the skirt had a split on both sides of her waist with an opening for her navel, and it was low cut to reveal her cleavage. Her makeup was perfect and the bruise was barely noticeable.

The room was exquisitely decorated, with a huge ice

sculpture of a man swinging a bat. Huge piles of shrimp, crab legs, cheese squares, and fruit surrounded the frozen, translucent figure. A champagne fountain sat next to the sculpture spewing what seemed like an endless amount of golden bubbly.

Michael held my hand continuously, even when we were sitting down. I must admit, we did look good and probably seemed like the perfect couple. However, as with anything made by man, there had to be some flaws. Remember when y'all were little and your grandmother would say things like, "Don't eat where you mess?" Well, by the looks of what was probably about to happen, I must've taken a massive dump all over my plate.

Damn . . .

"Look directly in front of you . . . a little to the left," Toi whispered in my ear.

When I looked up, I saw Fred staring at me looking hurt and disgusted. I looked him in his eyes and whispered under my breath so he could read my lips.

"Hi."

I wanted him to know that it didn't bother me to see him there. I wasn't gonna let him intimidate me, especially not when I was with my man. Even though he was with his wife, he couldn't hide the anger on his face.

He started to walk toward our table. I knew there was nothing to be concerned about, since Johnny and Fred were friends, and he knew Michael. The only thing that could be a problem would be his wife, if she were to recognize me. But, I didn't have time to worry about small stuff. Y'all know what I'm saying?

"What's up man?" he said as he gave Johnny a soulful handshake.

"Hi Toi and Candice. You both look beautiful tonight."

He then bent down and kissed both of us on our cheek. As he leaned in to kiss me, he whispered, "I need to talk to you." I continued to smile and pretended he'd said nothing.

Fred just nodded toward Michael and said, "What's up?"

He didn't bother to shake his hand. I grabbed Michael's hand and focused all of my attention on him, but as soon as I looked away from Fred he said to Toi, "So Toi, when did you and Candice get into town?"

Before Toi could answer, a reporter came over and wanted to speak with Michael. He stood up from the table.

"Baby, excuse me for a moment. I need to go and speak with this reporter for a few."

This was definitely one of those times when you know God is watching over you. My heart had started to beat a hundred miles a second before Michael got up. Fred was definitely trying to push my buttons.

I was relieved when he got up because I didn't know what Fred was trying to pull.

Toi hesitated. She looked at Johnny and then at me before she answered.

"We've been here for a few days, shopping, eating, doing things that women like to do."

"Why didn't y'all call me? You know I wanted to see you," Fred asked as he looked into my eyes.

Johnny looked puzzled. He was a good friend of both Michael and Fred. I knew he didn't want to be in the middle of our mess, so I said, "Fred, isn't that your lovely wife over there, what's her name? Didn't I meet her the last time I ran into you?"

He looked at me with fury in his eyes, but before he could answer me I said, "Toi will you please walk with me to the ladies' room?" We got up from the table and left.

"He's trippin' big time," Toi said as we headed toward the ladies' room.

"That nigga's with his wife. I don't think he'll be bothering us anymore."

"That man is obsessed with you girl. You done let him taste the candy, now he's lost his freakin' mind. He just walked to the table and started talking like he didn't even see Michael at all."

"I know that took a lot of nerve. I'm glad that reporter came over to speak with Michael, because ain't no telling what Fred would've said."

When we walked out of the ladies' room, Fred was waiting for me by the door. He pulled my arm and said, "What the hell do you think you are doing?!"

"Would you please let go of my arm? Leave me alone and go back to your wife."

"I asked you, what the hell are you doing? Is that faggot ass nigga getting my pussy?"

He squeezed my arm and pushed me up against the wall.

"Stop Fred! Let go of me!"

I tried to pull away from him, but he pushed me harder against the wall and said, "I asked you is that nigga gettin' what's mine?"

I did not acknowledge his question, I just kept trying to pull away from him.

"Candice, I love you. I'm not going to let you go that easy. Don't make me tell that nigga you wit who woman you really is."

I finally pushed past him and walked away. He was really trippin'.

What had I gotten myself into? He wanted me so bad that he'd do anything to mess up what I had. That nigga'd even risk his wife knowing what happened between us because he knew that she is not going nowhere. She has a proven track record that she is not leaving.

Toi asked all stupid while looking concerned, "Do you think you should tell Michael that you messed around with Fred before he does or before he finds out?"

"Hell no, I'm not going to tell him anything, and if Fred tells him I would deny most of it anyway. The sex was good, but it's not worth all this drama, especially if it means loosing my baby. Anyway, Fred has too much to lose. He is married to a woman he claims he don't love, because it will cost him too much to leave her. Why would he take a chance and mess up his situation, by telling Johnny, when he know that I don't want him?"

The rest of the night went by like a blur. Michael and I danced and laughed, but every now and then I'd catch Fred just staring. Remember that plate of mess I talked about earlier? I really had a mouthful right about now. But, as usual, you can never keep a true diva down.

After we left the party, Michael and I made passionate love all night. Afterward, I actually began to forget about the whole Fred thing. I just enjoyed my visit, and before we knew it, it was time to get back to reality again.

My trip to Atlanta was an eventful one this time. Toi and I accomplished all that we needed to. I really enjoyed Michael, and I knew now that nothing was more important than being with him. I didn't care if I ever saw Fred again. He was history. I made a mistake, but it'll never happen again.

Okay, okay, I am not a woman who never say never because never is a long word. I try not to say what I will never do so I'll just say that for now, I'm a one-man woman.

I always enjoyed seeing my baby in Atlanta, but there's no place like home. I was so happy when I set foot back in West Palm Beach. Amber was even on time to pick us up from the airport. She knows how I feel about having to wait after a long flight. I'm so impatient, but that's just me though. But my girl was at baggage claim waiting for us to arrive. She had a big smile on her face. Either Miss Lady was glad to see us, or she had something wonderful on her mind.

"What's up girl?" I asked as I gave her a hug.

"Did y'all divas have a good time in Atlanta? I wanted to join y'all, but I was so busy at work I couldn't get away."

"You weren't that busy at work. You were busy with that nigga. You must really be in love to turn down a free trip to Atlanta with you girls," Toi said jokingly.

"Did I miss anything important?"

"No. Ain't nothing more important than taking care of yo man. I'm sure you did that."

"Did y'all take care of that business with ol' boy?"

"We did what we had to do. You already know that Candice has an answer for everything. She hasn't let me down yet," Toi replied.

"She hasn't let you down? You mean she has never let me down. I don't know what I would do without her," Amber said as if I wasn't there.

"Would y'all stop talking about me like . . ."

Before I could finish my sentence, they both said, "We can't help if we love ya."

It feels good to have people love you and care about you. We were blessed to have each other. Besides Big Money, they were all the family that I had. My mom was murdered when I was fourteen and they never found out who did it. They really didn't try too hard because it happened in a crack house. My mom was one of the unlucky ones. She let crack ruin her life and eventually take it. She liked living fast. She was a beautiful woman, but didn't use it to her advantage. When I started high school, she began dating a big-time hustler. He turned her out on crack. She eventually lost her job, and I believe, most of her mind.

When her boyfriend caught a bullet, she couldn't support her habit anymore. Like most people who get hooked by drugs, she started doing anything and everything for a fix. Money told me she tried to win for a couple of dimes and was shot in the head. Although he had a nice crib, he stayed with me off and on at the apartment me and my mom lived in so I would not have to be by myself. I stayed in school because I knew that was my ticket out the hood. I had a job, but Money helped me pay the bills so I didn't have to go into a foster home. No one at school knew I lived alone at fifteen. My teachers thought that I had a family with a dog or something. I never let people know too much about me or my life.

I had no choice but to grow up if I wanted to survive that drug-infested environment. I was determined to make it, and, by the grace of God, I did. I had no other blood family in the world. This was why Toi and Amber's friendship was so important to me. I have always considered Money my family. I didn't have no one else until my girls came into my life.

Amber and Toi were getting too serious for me, so I changed the subject as we drove off.

"So Miss Thang, what did you do that was so important it kept you from coming to Atlanta?"

"Well, if you must know, I went out of town with Kenny."

"You didn't tell us you were going out of town when I called."

"I know. I didn't want y'all to worry or ask questions that I didn't have answers for."

"What did you do that would make us worry?"

At that moment, Amber got a serious look on her face. She looked at me, and then she stared at the floor of the car. She lifted her hand up and showed us her ring finger.

"I went to Lake Tahoe and got married."

Toi and I both started screaming and pulling her hand closer so we could see the ring. We hugged her and congratulated her on her marriage. Once she saw that we didn't question her decision, she started yelling and singing, "I'm married! I'm married! Amber got a man! Amber got her man!" She waved her hand in the air as if she was dancing to music.

We joined in with her, the best backup singers in the world.

"Amber's married! Amber's married! Amber got a husband. Go Amber. It's yo birthday, no Amber it's yo wedding day!"

"Girl, how does it feel?"

"When did y'all decide to get married?"

"How did he ask you?"

"Girl, we want to know everything."

We confused Amber with our barrage of questions. She turned her head from the left to the right and back again, not knowing which question to answer first. She decided to wait until we got to my house before she would say anything.

When we arrived at my house, Amber told us how they went for a walk in the park, and he started telling her how important she was to him. Then, out the blue, he got down on one knee and asked her to marry him. If you knew Amber you'd know that she probably fainted. At first she didn't know what to do, but they did know that they didn't want a big wedding. So, they eloped.

Amber is a good person, and she deserved a good man in her life. She's already acting like the perfect wife. As soon as we got to my house, she called her new hubby and told him that she was going to sit with me for a while and she'd be home in about an hour. When she hung the phone up, Toi said teasingly, "You act like you've had practice at this. You calling and thangs, reporting in with yo man like a good wife should."

"She's doing the right thing. Girl, don't pay no attention to her. Anyway Toi, you report your every move to Johnny. It's just respect. That's what makes a good relationship. You supposed to let your man know that you're thinking about him. A man feels more secure when he knows where his woman is and what she's doing. But, remember, a nigga still needs to know only so much."

We talked for over an hour before Amber went home. Toi stayed with me while I unpacked my clothes. This gave us a chance to talk about all that happened in Atlanta. When I finished with my clothes, we decided to call it a day and meet for dinner tomorrow after work. So, I took her home.

FOURTEEN

Is it for love, financial security, or the sex?
Can you honor the commitment?
Why do you want me at your disposal?
Think before the ring and . . .

the proposal

Michael had had a long and tiring month. His team had been traveling nonstop for the past three weeks, only to come home for two home stands that lasted two days each time. Being away from my man for a whole month was not in this program, at least, not the one that I was directing. Anything over two weeks apart, the script has to be rewritten. I needs mine. My man is way too good to me and I miss him way too much to stay away from him for too long. Besides, I be missing my baby too much.

To solve our problem of him traveling all month, I decided to meet him on the road. I was waiting for him when he arrived in San Francisco with nothing on but a red bow tied around the hairs on my paradise. Oh yeah, he knew I was coming to meet him. I'd never surprise my man like that. I don't want to be the one to get the surprise, if you know what I mean. I know a couple of women who showed up without their man knowing. One of them caught her husband with his head buried deep between another woman's legs when she opened the door. Who do you think got the biggest surprise out of that situation?

The other woman came into town earlier than her man expected and slipped on something sexy. When she heard him coming, she hid in the closet and was planning on jumping out and saying, "Surprise!"

Before she could, she heard a woman's voice. To see what was going on, she decided to stay in the closet and listen. To her surprise, it wasn't one woman, but two. The three of them had a nasty freak party. While one girl was sucking him, he was licking the other's cat and butt hole while she bent over. Now peep this, she had her finger in his butt at the same time. Eww wee baby, now that's just too nasty. He didn't even wipe himself off between changes, and the women just loved it. He even screwed them in the butt. I already told y'all how I felt about that dookie love. Can you imagine having a nigga that nasty? What's worse, what if he's yo husband? You would have a mess on your hands and you would not even know it. This makes me wonder, does any-one ever really know their mate or who they are sleeping with every night?

Every time I visit my man, he knows that I'm coming. I'm not trying to get surprised. I don't want him popping up on me, and I won't be popping up on him.

When I met him in St. Louis, I made sure that I'd arrive on his off day. I wanted him to pick me up from the airport. When he saw me walking through the airport terminal, he had that "I'm going to tap that ass" look in his eyes. He gave me a big hug, and acted like he didn't want to let me go. So, while we were waiting on my luggage, I took his hand and put it under my dress. All he felt was this hot wetness between my legs. That nigga got an instant hard-on and rushed me to the limo. Before I sat down good, he was all in me, and I was lovin' every inch of it.

That's the kind of response I like getting from my man. I love doing unexpected freaky stuff like this. A man loves it and it definitely helps to spice up a relationship. Like I keep tellin' y'all, tease then please and you can live yo life with ease.

We'd become inseparable. It was like we're totally connected. Even though we had not seen each other in a month we still talked every day. We really tried to understand each other's wants, dislikes, and pet peeves. I was not trying to change him, and he was not trying to change me. We accepted each other fully, even though we might not agree all the time. That's okay though. A mature relationship means not being afraid to let your mate be his or her own person.

Michael told me that he couldn't deal with our situation, us being apart, for much longer. I felt the same way. Sometimes after I've had a long hard day, I just want my man to put his arms around me and hold me. I want to be able to roll over in the middle of the night and get mine when I'm ready. I like to get mine even when my man is asleep. I turn him on his back and ride it. He may be asleep when I start, but before the second or third stroke he's wide awake.

We liked spending all our free time together, but our schedules just wouldn't allow it. Yeah . . . I know, but sometimes ya gotta do what ya gotta do to be where ya wanna be. So, I've started to make time for my relationship. My time is a little more flexible because I set my own hours.

I often wonder how ballplayers' wives deal with their husbands' being away from home most of the year. Nah, I gotta be real with y'all. The wives that are in it for the financial security don't care if the nigga ever come home. They don't want to be bothered with him anyway.

In fact, one of Michael's teammate's wives told me that she likes when her husband is gone because she cannot stand to be around him too long. But check this out, she said that when he touches her she feels nasty and that she doesn't like making love to him at all. She's boning his cousin anyway. Now, that's some foolish there. Well, it is her life and I can't judge a woman for doing what she thinks she has to do to keep her sanity.

For the women that actually love their man, they really have problems. The distance is nothing compared to all the hoes looking for a sugar daddy. Y'all already know what I'm talkin' about. That's the broads that follow the team from city to city and state to state fucking, sucking, and doing whatever it takes to get a man. I can't see it. This is one of the reasons why a relationship has to have a solid foundation. The wives have so much to deal with, but the nigga always think that the money compensates for all of the extra bull.

People think that because a woman is married to a player, all of her worries and hard times disappear. They believe that she lives a fairy-tale life and that all her dreams come true, but nothing can be further from the truth.

First of all, a professional ballplayer has two lives that are completely opposite one another: the world of sports and family.

His sports life consists of fame, notoriety, women, sex, groupies, and of course, the game itself, which he loves more than life.

Then, there is his family, which consists of his wife and/or kids. He tries to appreciate his family because subconsciously he knows he needs them. In reality, his career and the fast-paced lifestyle keep him on a high. It's a natural high that money can't buy, nor can it be understood unless you have experienced it for yourself. He has unlimited access to a life that most men only dream about.

When he can't get this high at home because he's caught up in the hype and he doesn't understand the value of family, he does the inevitable. He gets the groupie who has screwed most of the players in the leagues and makes her his mistress. A one-night stand is different from a mistress. When yo man screws a woman for one night and forgets about her, that's a one-night stand. When he starts breaking her off something proper, that hoe has become a mistress. And he thinks, as long as his wife don't know, that he is not doing any wrong.

If the player is weak-minded, pussy-led, and don't have no morals, he'll make that same hoe that's been with most of his friends his wife. Ain't that a bitch?

What's funny about that whole situation is that anything is good when you're creeping. It's surreal, a fantasy. When all of the sneaking ain't a game no more, it becomes something you must deal with every single day. Reality sinks in, and the player realizes that the grass he thought was greener on the other side is only turf, a cheap substitute that could never replace the real thing—the original Mrs.

When he wakes up, his true love is gone and the nigga is unhappy. But he is still trying to convince himself and others that he made the right decision.

On the other hand, the life of a ballplayer's wife revolves around her man. She waits for him to come home, so they can talk about his day. Instead of getting the affection she so desperately needs, she's confronted with nothing but his emptiness.

He can't understand why she's so unhappy when he's provided her with all of the finest things in life that money can buy. What he fails to understand is that he's her total life, but she knows that she's only a small part of his. How can a woman be happy knowing everything and everybody comes before her in their marriage? And y'all wonder why these marriages don't last. Some folks are just too messed up in the head, just plain stupid.

Anyway, Michael made me promise him that I'd be in Atlanta waiting for him when he returned from his latest road trip. Of course I was gonna be there. I couldn't stay away from my man too long. He has his needs and I surely have mine. Believe that!

During the last two months, Fred had called me a lot. He would go from talking all sweet to cursing me out.

I got so tired of him bothering and worrying me that I changed all my phone numbers. He refused to believe that I was in love and that I wasn't sitting around waiting for him. Even though I knew he wanted me, that fool couldn't give me what I needed in a relationship. And . . . um . . . I'm no hater or nothing, but I'm not trying to share the man I'm in love with. I'm not trying to share him with nobody.

Toi and Johnny had set a date for their wedding. I was so happy for her. They were truly in love and enjoyed each other's company. I just hoped Johnny had totally given up his extracurricular activities. Sometimes old habits are hard to break.

Toi had been getting a lot of crazy phone calls. When she picked up the phone, all she'd hear was some heavy breathing. Sometimes, whoever the pervert was on the other end just hung up when she said "hello." It got so bad that she had to call the police because the muffled voice on the other end said, "You dead bitch." Like I told my girl, I don't know. She'd better just be careful.

My flight arrived in the Atlanta airport forty-five minutes before Michael's flight. After the limo driver retrieved my luggage, he drove me to the baggage claim where Michael would exit.

"I missed you so much," Michael said with much sincerity. His arms were my sanctuary. When I was there, I had no worries. If I could package that feeling and sell it, I'd be a billionaire a million times over. Most people look for that feeling all their lives, but only a very few find it. I consider it a blessing.

"Where are we going baby?" I asked.

"You'll see soon enough, my love," he replied.

I didn't inquire any further. I just enjoyed the ride.

We pulled up in front of my favorite restaurant, Sanders Supper Club. My smile told him how excited and pleased I was. Sanders Supper Club is an upscale restaurant that has the best fried lobster that I've ever tasted. The ambiance is mellow, and the customer service is great.

As we entered the restaurant, the maître d' escorted us to a secluded room in the back of the restaurant. The room was full of beautiful exotic floral arrangements and roses of various colors. I mean . . . the entire room was full of the flowers, and in the left corner sat a baby grand piano. A pianist was playing and singing, "One in a Million."

"Baby you know that I love you and I can't imagine living the rest of my life without you in my life," Michael said.

Then he handed me a white rose. "Baby, this white rose symbolizes the purity of the love that I have for you. I love and accept you completely and would never try to change who you are."

He lifted my hands and kissed them softly. Then he just sat there for a few seconds staring at me without saying a word.

He picked up a pink rose and handed it to me. "This pink rose symbolizes how beautiful you are to me. I'm not talking about your physical beauty . . ."

He stopped for a minute and softly touched my face. Then he traced my lips with the tip of his fingers. "I'm talking about your inner beauty. How you always put me and others before yourself. Always wanting to please everyone and make them happy, doing this all without compromising your self-respect or self-esteem."

He handed me a red rose. "This red rose symbolizes all the love in my heart that I have for you. It symbolizes how much you mean to me and that I want to share all of me with you. You are a part of me and without you, I'm not whole. I need you to be a part of my life. I need your love, your touch and all the mental stimulation that you give me. When I'm down you always know it. I don't have to tell you when I don't want to be bothered, you just lie next to me and don't say anything. I love you for that and for trying to understand my ways. I know that I'm not perfect and probably will never be. But I do know that I love you and want you to be my wife."

He hesitated and stared deeply into my eyes. "Candice, you're the one and only woman for me. I'd be honored if you would be my lady for life. What I'm trying to say . . . is will you marry me?"

When I was finally able to see through the tears that flooded my eyes, I looked down at the rose he had handed me and that's when I saw an engagement ring hanging from one of the stems. Tears were streaming down my face while my hands shook uncontrollably as I tried to get the ring.

Michael noticed that I was too nervous to get the ring off the stem, so he reached over and got the ring, bent down on one knee and said again, "Baby, I love you. I love you more than anything in this world. I want us to spend the rest of our lives together as one. I want us to raise a family together. Oh baby, I love you so much . . . Will you marry me?"

I couldn't stop crying because I was so happy. The greatest man in the world, whom I love, adore, and admire, had just asked me to be his wife. My heart was saying yes, but my mouth wasn't moving.

Finally, I got control and whispered, "Yes."

He slipped the ring on my finger, picked me up out of the chair and started turning me around laughing and saying, "She said yes! She said yes! Thank you Jesus!"

Suddenly, the doors opened and all of our friends walked in. I was so surprised to see them.

Toi, Johnny, Amber, and everybody else yelled, "Congratulations!"

Toi and Amber hugged me while Amber said, "I guess all three of us will be old married pregnant ladies soon." We all laughed and reached out for our men.

"Old, I can't agree with that shit," I said.

"I can't agree with that old shit either. I am too damn fine and sexy," Toi stated.

"Hey, I guess the OAD Club is one deep," I said.

"OAD? What the hell is that?" Johnny asked.

"Old Ass Diva," I replied with a big smile.

This was really a surprise. They really kept it all from me. I didn't even know Toi and Amber were in Atlanta. I was so glad that they were here to help me celebrate my engagement to Michael.

I was about to take the plunge again. After years of being alone—notice I didn't say lonely— I'm ready to give myself to a man. A man who I would be honored to spend the rest of my life with. Besides meeting Michael, this had to be one of the best days in my life.

During the course of the evening, we decided that we'd have a double wedding: Johnny, Toi, Michael, and myself. This decision would give Toi and me even more to talk about. I couldn't wait to start planning for the big day.

When we left the restaurant, one of Johnny's tires was

slashed and both sides of his car had been keyed. We looked around, but didn't see anybody. I felt as if someone was watching us.

Toi had something similar happen to her back in Florida, but this was Atlanta. Maybe it was all just a coincidence.

Michael and Johnny changed the tire. They couldn't think of a reason why someone would do that to Johnny's car. I know Toi probably thought that it might be another woman, even though she didn't say so.

After we got tired of talking about why it might have happened, Toi and Johnny left and we headed for Michael's house.

The season would be over in October. We decided to have the wedding the following June. We only had a few months to plan the perfect double wedding, and I sure was looking forward to it.

FIFTEEN

I did it
It's done
I can't fret
It was a learning experience
So I have . . .

no regrets

Time moves so fast. Can you believe that it was only two days before I was to be married? I thought that I'd be scared to death by then, but I'd managed to keep my cool. Maybe because this was the day that most women dream about, walking down an aisle into the life of a good man. If you ask me, I'm the luckiest woman in the world.

Since I never really knew my no-good-for-nothin' dad who lived only twenty minutes from me, I asked Big Money, my closest friend in the world, to walk me down the aisle.

When I look at Big Money, I see years of love there. I love him, and I know that he loves me. He's been more than a friend for the last twenty-seven years of my life. He has had the leading male role in my life's story for as long as I can remember. Anything that a man can be for a woman, he's been for me. Money has managed to be my brother, father, lover, friend, confidant, and security blanket. Through all of the different stages in my life, we've still found a way to maintain our loyalty, love, and trust for each other.

It's kind of hard to believe, but he's finally let the street game go. At one time, he owned most of the old houses on Rosemary Avenue, where we grew up. He had over twenty blocks of housing and commercial developments. When I say this, I mean he actually held the titles to these buildings.

Money has always been a smart man. He used to have this big-time attorney representing him who had an office in Palm Beach. While waiting to meet with his attorney one day, he overheard him talking to one of the city officials from West Palm Beach. They were talking about revitalizing the whole downtown area and getting rid of the old buildings. They even had drawings of the new downtown district.

After thorough checking, he confirmed what he heard. He knew if he acted fast it'd benefit him in the long run. He didn't tell a soul but me. He said that it was a blessing that he heard that information and he had to take advantage of it. Money, being a true hustler, heard opportunity knocking and let it in.

Coming from the streets, he knew the owners wanted to sell their houses, but no one was biting because the neighborhood had gotten so rundown. Can you imagine you and your kids having to live next to a dilapidated crack house full of junkies?

It didn't take Money long to start his campaign. He went to every owner and personally made him or her an offer. Of course the owners sold out. Once they realized that Money had bought all of the old houses, they thought he'd lost his mind. They assumed that he was going to turn the neighborhood into a "crackville" or something.

When the city started buying up the avenue in order to extend certain roads, combine others, and build high-rise hotels to accommodate the tourists, Money held out longer than any other owner. He owned the properties that sat dead in the middle of the city's plans. The city had to do whatever it took to purchase the land, or they'd have had to start all over again. When the legal wrangling was over, he cleared a settlement worth over 150 million dollars for the sale of his properties, and yours truly is his money manager.

He doesn't have to worry about finances anymore because he's set for life. After he got his money, he decided to leave West Palm Beach. He realized that he'd gotten tired of the fast life. The only person he took with him was his boy, Black. He moved to a small town around 150 miles outside of Atlanta. He stopped going by Big Money and used his real name, Reginald Johnson. He said he just wanted to meet a good woman, have some children, and enjoy the rest of his life without all the drama. I was proud to have him give me away.

I made all of the last-minute phone calls and arrangements. I wanted to make sure that everyone knew what they were supposed to do. I had to confirm all the deliveries, approve the menu, and finalize the play list with the DJ. When I couldn't contact his hyper butt, I went into a small panic, but Toi assured me that I didn't have to worry, because she had spoken with him already.

The hair stylist was trippin' 'cause she said I wanted her there earlier than what the contract said, and I had to pay her more. I had to explain to her that the only thing I was going to pay her was a kick in her nasty behind if she was not there at the time I said. I had already paid her in full and told her that I'd tip her 20 percent of the agreed-upon price once she finished, and she was still acting stupid. She got the message, though, and cleaned up all of the dumb talk.

I went over my list more than once. Toi kept telling me to relax, but I couldn't. I had to make sure that everything was going as planned.

I was trying not to think too much about the actual ceremony. When I did, memories of two girls I once knew kept popping in my head.

One of the girls was seeing a guy for around six months. They spent three days a week together. They both worked and had responsibilities, so it was hard seeing each other every day. He asked her to marry him and told her he had the ring on layaway. He even took her by the jeweler to see it. She was so happy. She told everyone right away that she was going to get married. Girl, she had even started planning the wedding.

Two months into the engagement, she was sitting at breakfast with her mom reading the Sunday paper. She was the kind of person that liked to gossip about other people's business, so she turned to the Wedding Announcement section to see the latest victims. This section highlighted the previous month's newlyweds by showing them on their wedding day. As soon as she turned to the pages to view all of the pictures, guess whose picture was the first one she saw? BAM! Damn right. Her fiancé, without a ring, had just gotten married the week before.

A nigga ain't shit. He didn't even tell her that he was seeing someone else. She had just stayed the night with him two nights before his wedding day, and he didn't act suspicious at all.

Now check this out. When she called me crying, I told her to call him and act like she don't know and see what he'd say. How 'bout the Negro changed all his numbers and moved out of his apartment. She didn't even know that he'd moved.

As I said before, a nigga ain't shit.

The most messed-up thing is that the whole situation made her into a hoe. She started humping every man she met to get over him. To this day, she's somewhere being a tramp, still alone and brokenhearted.

A woman can't let a man get her so down to where she loses all of her self-respect. Sometimes shit happens, you just have to deal with it. I've learned that's what being a woman is all about, holding your ground and never giving up.

I knew this other chick who just wanted to be married. She just wanted a husband and would do anything to get one. She didn't care whose man he was. Hey, she'd have taken your man, my man, her momma's man, anybody's man; she just didn't want to be alone. She was infatuated with the idea of love and marriage.

Well anyway, she finally found this fool that agreed to marry her. Yeah, yeah she asked him. I said that she was desperate.

They set the date and she spent her life's savings on putting the wedding together.

I had to give it to her, the crazy fool had good taste, and everything was beautiful.

On their wedding day, everyone was in the church talking about how everything was well put together. When the music started playing, she stepped into the aisle on her father's arm. She started strutting, moving gracefully and elegantly. The crazy witch was a beautiful bride. Gotta give props where props are due. All eyes were on her; like I said, I ain't a hater. She may have been stupid, but she didn't look stupid.

Honey, by the time she made it to the end of the aisle, her man had disappeared. First, she stood there anxiously, not knowing what to do. She acted like he had just gone to the bathroom or something and would be right back.

For an hour, she stood there with her father and wouldn't move. Neither would she let her father move. She just clung to him tightly like a small child would do when he was scared.

Once most of the guests had gone, she just sat on the floor at the altar and started crying. Her father had to pick her up and carry her out of the church. She cried for weeks at a time and wouldn't eat. She started to look like she was really crazy. She used to act like she was, but now she looked like she was, too. In fact, she was the exact opposite of the girl that we just finished talking about.

Ultimately, the pain and hurt, along with the embarrassment of him leaving her, caused her to take a bottle of pills. When they found her dead on her bedroom floor, she had her wedding dress on.

I never saw the old boy again. You know, the dude that left her standing at the altar? I guess after she killed herself, he couldn't face anyone who he thought she knew. Somebody told me he moved to Seattle.

I'd been praying that our wedding day would be a day to remember. I prayed that everything would go as planned and that it would be a perfect ceremony, one that would be talked about for years and years to come. Toi and I would be there, and hopefully our men would show up. But just in case the niggas wanted to act a little stupid, I got a .22 with a couple of bullets for their asses.

SIXTEEN

When I married you
I knew there would be some hurt
But I made the commitment . . .

for better or worse

Well, today was the big day.. This was the beginning of the rest of my life, and I was ready to get it started. Toi was in the next room getting dressed. She acted like she didn't have a nervous bone in her body. I was so nervous that my body fluids kept doing their own thang. I'd been shittin' and showering all morning. I got tired of jumping in the shower every time I would use the bathroom, so I got some baby wipes to keep with me. A woman don't want to be smelling like shit on her big day. Damn, I hoped it was just nerves and not the runs.

As I put on my wedding attire, I thought about how far I'd grown emotionally. There was a time when I would've never allowed myself to love another man the way I loved Michael. I would've never let a man get to my heart the way he had. I never wanted to need a man emotionally, because it's the worst need of all.

See, needing someone financially is easy to handle. If that need isn't met, you move on to the one that can give you the financial security that you desire. But emotions aren't something that you always have control over. They don't just come and go. They can't just be traded in for the next nigga or relationship.

You know what? It's scary knowing that you are depending on hearing from someone just to make your day complete and when you don't hear from that certain someone you feel empty inside, like something is missing.

I never wanted to have my mental stability depend on an uncontrollable dependence, because feelings, whether love or hate, come and go with the wind. Anyway, feelings are too unpredictable. They will have you doing things you thought you never would do. To me, anything that strong can be very dangerous. I don't give a damn what it is.

With Michael, we had a mutual respect for each other. I was glad I waited for love. I've had other proposals from men with money, but I wanted more. I wanted it all, and now I had it.

I listened to those wives who talk about how they like it when their husbands leave or go away on a trip. They can't stand for him to touch 'em or make love to them. Some even cringe when their husbands try to kiss or hold them. I never wanted to deal with that feeling just for the money. The money has never been an issue. I know how to make my own. Don't get me wrong, my man has to have financial security. Although I'm not hurting for cash, I must know that my man can take care of me, if needed.

Like I said before, I want the love and the money. I want it all! I've always wanted that special feeling that I'd found with Michael.

I waited because I wanted the kind of love where I want my man so much that when he leaves, he takes a part of me with him. What keeps me going while he is away from me is that I know he'll be back soon for his other half and when he gets back everything will be all good. That was the feeling I got with Michael and I would cherish it always.

Well, Toi and I were ready to take what was hopefully our final walk as single women. I don't know why, but every episode of *Sex and the City* flashed through my head before I snapped back to the present moment. Damn, I guess TV does play a major role in the way we think. I heard the music playing. I could feel it in my bones. I listened carefully because when Patti started to sing, that was our cue. Toi was walking down a separate aisle, but we'll meet at the end.

When Patti started to sing and I stepped out into the aisle, my heart started racing a mile a minute.

I tried to take my first step, but my leg wouldn't move. I just stood there. I tried to move my foot again but nothing happened. For some strange reason, I started breathing fast as if I was about to hyperventilate.

"Don't do it! Run! There's the exit to your left, just go through it! You don't have to worry about anything else. Run! Don't look back," a voice kept repeating in my mind.

My legs started wobbling, and I looked up at the exit. "Run, while you still have a chance," the voice continued to say.

I looked at the exit again and then I looked down the aisle, and I saw Michael standing at the altar. He was smiling, waiting patiently for his woman to join him. When I looked into his eyes and saw the confidence he had in me and in our relationship and I felt all the love he felt for me, I knew that with him was where I belonged. As our eyes locked, he whispered as I read his lips, "I love you, baby." I knew then that I was not going to let anything stop me from getting to where I belonged.

My heart slowed down, my panting stopped, and my legs became lighter. I took my first step knowing that I was walking toward my new life. The life I'd waited for all of my days, and the perfect man to share it with. A man I loved and adored.

I finally made it to the altar. Toi made it to Johnny. He was grinning like he'd just won the Lotto. Toi looked beautiful as usual with a big smile on her face.

"We are gathered here today . . ." the preacher started speaking. As he continued, I looked deep into Michael's eyes and felt his energy. I could feel his excitement and happiness.

Michael and I wrote our own vows. When the preacher stopped, I knew that it was time for me to say what I had written for Michael.

"I love you Michael. I love you more than life itself. I promise you that I'll be the best wife and friend that the Lord allows me to be, and I promise to try to be understanding in all aspects of our lives together. I promise to love and cherish you from this day forward. It's taken me all my life to find you, and I promise that I'll do everything in my power to keep you happy, to keep us happy and together as one. I promise not to run out when things become tough because at times I know that they will. I will honor you and cherish you for as long as we both shall live."

"Candice, I promise to be the best husband that I know

how to be. I promise you that I'll not try to change you, but love you for who you are. I promise to stay open for any change that I may need to keep us happy and growing together as one. I promise you that I will not run out on you if things get hard and that I will always be there for you, loving you, giving you the security that a husband should give his wife. I promise to love you, honor you, and cherish you for as long as we both shall live."

As we kissed, I felt a connection with Michael that I prayed would last a lifetime. I felt as if the final piece of the puzzle was finally in place.

I looked over at Toi and Johnny and felt their excitement and happiness. Toi and I hugged each other and I said, "We finally did it, and it feels so damn good."

We walked down the aisle with our husbands smiling from ear to ear. The guests were reaching out to touch us, congratulating us and clapping as we walked by them.

"GOD BLESS YOU, and GOOD LUCK!" someone yelled.

When the church doors opened, the sun shone through brightly. It was a perfect sunny day for a wedding. As we walked, the guests started throwing rice.

Toi and I stopped to throw our flowers . . .

"NO! NO!" someone yelled.

The guests started pushing each other and running fast.

"STOP! He has a gun!"

The crowd went frantic, knocking each other down as they trampled each other. When I looked up I saw Toby coming from behind the church. At first, I did not notice the gun in his hand.

"NOOOOO!" Toi screamed.

As I heard Toi screaming at the top of her lungs, I looked at her and then looked over to where she was pointing. I saw Toby pointing the gun and I saw the flash of light coming from the gun.

"Oh my God, Toi watch out," I screamed at the top of my lungs.

Toby was pointing the gun right at Toi, but Johnny stepped in front of her. The crowd scattered, people were running up and down. They ducked behind whatever they thought could give them cover.

All I could see was the gush of blood that spattered all over Toi's white dress. I did not know if the bullet had hit Toi or Johnny. As I stood there in disbelief trying to see through the frantic crowd, Big Money grabbed me and pulled me down behind a fountain statue.

I saw Michael looking for me frantically. Money grabbed him and pointed me out to him. "Go take care of my girl, and I'll handle this."

I was still looking at Johnny and Toi. When I saw who the bullet had hit, I screamed.

"Johnny's been shot, Johnny's been shot. Watch out, he still has the gun!"

The bullet had hit Johnny in the middle of his heart, and blood gushed out everywhere.

Toby was still standing in front of them looking crazy, with the gun still in his hand. When he realized that he had shot Johnny instead of Toi he started crying while saying, "Bitch, see what you made me do. I didn't mean to do that Johnny, I'm sorry, I'm sorry. I did not want to hurt you, I wanted to . . ."

He stopped crying and pointed the gun at Toi.

Toi yelled, "NO! NO! GOD NO! Please don't do this to me. Please, please please."

She continued to say this as she reached for Johnny and pulled him closer to her. I looked at Toby and he was pointing the gun at Toi, but before he could pull the trigger, Big Money pulled out a gun and unloaded. Big Money might have left the street game, but the streets were still part of him. That he had his protection with him at all times was not surprising.

"BLAM! BLAM! BLAM!"

Toby fell to the ground with the gun still in his hand. Toi jumped up and started kicking him in the head while she said "Why, Toby?! Why did you do this to me?! You took my husband from me, you took my life! Why couldn't you just leave us alone?! Why!"

Michael grabbed her and pulled her over to where I was. She was still screaming at Toby. I tried to calm her down, but it didn't help. She kept crying and screaming at the top of her lungs.

"Why, Candice? Why did he do this to us? Why? Why, Candice, why?"

I didn't know what to do or say. I tried to calm her down again, but she was too hysterical. I felt so sorry for her and yet still I knew there wasn't anything that I could do to take her pain away. This was one of the few times that I didn't have the answers.

All I heard was the ringing of gunshots in my ears, "BLAM! BLAM! BLAM!" Toi was still screaming uncontrollably and the crowd was shocked with disbelief.

When I looked up, Big Money and his boy Black were

taking all the tapes from the cameras and the video equipment. They also took all the photographers' film.

He ran over to me and said, "Red, me and my man have to bounce before the police come. Take care of your girl, and I'll be in touch."

He disappeared in a matter of seconds. All I kept hearing in my head was the gunshots, the screaming, Toi crying, and the sirens from the ambulance and police cars.

I kept waiting to wake up because I knew this had to be a dream. Please, God let me wake up, I knew this couldn't be real. But as I touched myself and felt the wetness from the blood that was on Toi's dress and face, I knew that it was real and there was nothing that I could do to change it.

This was supposed to be the most beautiful and joyous day of our lives and it ended in a tragedy that would affect each one of us in one way or another.

SEVENTEEN

Life ain't fair and it never will be
The adversity built my character
Brought me closer to me,
My character prepared me for success
It helped me to weather the storms
And wouldn't let me settle for less,
Life ain't fair and it never will be
So why you still jealous
Envious and hatin' on me,
I have been through the struggle
But that part you can not see
Wishing I don't succeed
Hoping that I'm unhappy,
Life ain't fair and it never will be
So every morning I pray
Lord please help me through another day
Lord I need a blessing
Please throw one my way,
Every night I pray
Lord thank you for being with me
Thank you for my health, strength, and family
Thank you for the endurance you've given me
To deal with . . .

life ain't fair. . . and it never will be

ood morning sweetheart," I said to Michael as he walked into the kitchen.

"Good morning my beautiful angels," he replied as he smiled and kissed me on my lips. He kissed Mykyla on her forehead.

Yeah, I'm still living a fairy-tale life with Michael. We get along so well that every day seems like a minivacation. Our marriage is almost perfect. I can't think of a serious argument we've ever had. In the beginning, can you believe that your girl used to wait for something bad to happen? Everything was so perfect, I just knew that it would not last. Eventually, though, I accepted the fact that we're meant to be together. That's when I decided not to create or wait for problems that don't exist. If you think about it, most of us are drama queens. We've become so used to problems that we create our own drama just to have something to complain about.

Michael and I disagree sometimes, but since both of us are so easygoing it hasn't escalated into nothing major. We are definitely soulmates. I know what he is thinking before he says it and he knows how I feel without me explaining.

I've finally figured out the key to making a relationship work and last: Both people have to want it. There must be mutual respect, communication, and both of you must have an open mind. Both people must also try to understand what has been communicated. They must be able to trust each other and should not smother each other because of insecurity. Spending all of their free time together is good, but only if they both enjoy each other's time and not because they are trying to keep track of each other's whereabouts. Remember, everybody needs some space every now and then.

You must love each other, but that is not the key ingredient. The key ingredient to a successful relationship is "adoration." When you adore someone, you like everything about that person. The way he walks is sexy, the way he holds his fork is cute, and if he just happens to spill something on your new dress it's funny to you, because you never knew he could be so clumsy. Yeah, when you adore someone you surpass love, because there isn't much the person can do that you won't find cute or find a way to admire.

Just when I thought our marriage couldn't get any better, I was proven wrong. Since the birth of our baby girl, Mykyla, who is thirteen months old, our relationship has become so good that it really scares me to think about how much in love we are. Mykyla is a beautiful little girl and she looks just like her daddy. She has the same hair I had when I was a child, big curly locks. Her skin is pecan tan, which is a combination of both of our complexions. We've been trying to have a second child; Michael wants a son. I've been feeling funny this past week, so let's just keep our fingers crossed.

I cook eggs, pancakes, cheese grits, and sausage. Michael always likes a good breakfast because he usually eats only fruit for lunch. He doesn't like to practice or play on a full stomach. He thinks that it slows him down.

"Patty cake, patty cake, baker's man," Michael sang to Mykyla as he clapped her hands together.

He keeps a smile on her face and on mine. He really works hard to make us happy. When Mykyla sees her father, she reaches out with a grin from ear to ear. She's truly a "daddy's girl."

As I look at my beautiful family, I think about how blessed I am. For years Big Money, Toi, and Amber have been the only family I've had. Now I have a respectable husband, a healthy baby girl, and a beautiful marriage. What more can a woman ask for? Well money, we have that too. So there's definitely no complaining on this end.

Life has finally dealt me a decent hand, one that I can work with. I'd feel guilty if I asked for any more than I have now. When I think about it, the only thing that's missing in my life is my relationship with Toi.

It's been two years since the shooting, and I haven't really talked to Toi since that day. After the ambulance took Johnny to the hospital, only to be pronounced dead, Toi seemed to lose a little bit of her sanity. She wouldn't respond when people spoke to her. She just sat in her chair staring at the hospital walls. She didn't even go to identify her husband's body. I had to do it. I tried to take her home, but she wouldn't go. Amber and I ended up sitting with her for hours in the private waiting room of the hospital.

At that time I had a sharp piercing pain run through my heart. I felt guilty about the happiness I had by being Michael's wife. Wow . . . think about it. What if it had been Michael instead of Johnny? I really don't know how I would have reacted, but I know that I'd be crazy right about now.

Toi and Johnny were a perfect match. I don't care what kind of extra activities he had going on. She'd waited all her life for a man like him, just to have him taken away over something dumb. I was in real pain, because I couldn't do anything to ease Toi's agony. I could only imagine how devastated she was. One minute she was happier then she thought she could ever be. She was living the dream that she thought would never come true. The next the carpet was pulled from under her and she landed right on her back wondering why in the hell she had to wake up. Life is a motha.

Damn, I wished there was something that I could've done to ease my girl's pain. The emptiness that I saw in her eyes scared the hell out of me. It wasn't a look of hurt, but one of revenge. But who would she get back at? Toby was already dead. Was she mad at the world? Did she still want to live?

She sat and looked at the walls without paying attention to her surroundings. There wasn't a thing that I could do to bring her out of that state of shock. I just sat with her and held her close to me. I didn't say a word for hours. The only voice I heard was the paging of doctors over the hospital's intercom system.

After hours of sitting and holding her in silence, I got up to go use the bathroom. When I came back, Toi was gone. I asked Amber where she went and she said, "To the bathroom." I was so pissed off at Amber. I couldn't understand why she'd let Toi go to the bathroom by herself. She knew that Toi was trippin'.

When she didn't come back within five minutes, I knew something was wrong. We checked every single bathroom on that floor, but we did not find her. At that point, I knew she was gone.

The last time I'd seen Toi was when I left her sitting in that chair. I didn't have a chance to talk her into staying or let her know how much I needed her in my life. It just hurt so damn much not to have my girl with me.

Six months after she left, I received a postcard from Toi. It had a Canadian postmark on it. A few months after that, I received another with a postmark from Paris. She never included a return address, and they had the same words, "Thinking about ya, love ya." I've received postcards from California, Spain, Russia, Florida, and Georgia. I guess that's her way of letting me know that she's thinking about me. I know she still hasn't dealt with her loss. If she had, she'd have come home by now. I ride by Johnny's house sometimes, hoping to see her there, but I never do. The housekeeper is living there and caring for things while she's away. When I stopped a few months back, to speak to the housekeeper, she said that she doesn't see Toi much. However, she added that Toi does send her paychecks on time.

I've really missed her these past two years. Why couldn't she just let me help her get through this? I know she needs me, but she still won't call. I know she still loves her girl, but I just wish she was here.

She sent Mykyla a present after she was born. The card read, *"To the most beautiful and precious baby in the world. I love u, your Aunt Toi."* Over the last year Mykyla has been periodically receiving presents in the mail from Toi. She has gotten everything from baby dolls to motorized cars.

It's funny, although I haven't heard from her she's still a part of our life. Toi's whole ordeal shows that just when you start to think that life's good, something unexpected happens to make you realize that life ain't fair and it never will be. You just have to get used to the hurt, pain, and disappointment, then figure out a way to keep going in spite of it all.

My business, Money Makers, is still growing and is very profitable. My marriage has opened a lot of doors for me. Michael is well-connected, not to mention that he's one of the best in his profession. I moved my main office to Atlanta. Also ya girl has been very busy makin' that money. Besides the branch in West Palm Beach, I opened up branches in Miami, Chicago, and New York. I'm working on opening up an office in Los Angeles. The only thing holding me back is that I can't seem to come to terms with the girl that would be managing the West Coast. I've added a couple of sports agents to the staff, and the athletes have taken full advantage of them. I'm currently working on this big deal with one of Atlanta's wealthiest men, Tony Machenski. He's part owner of the professional hockey team and owns several malls throughout the state.

Big Money still hasn't found that perfect woman. He says he wants a women like me, but I always joke and I say, "there ain't no more out there like me." He is the big man in the small town where he lives. He's started a nonprofit organization that helps underprivileged kids with homework and helps them prepare for college. The program makes sure that the school applications and financial grant applications are completed correctly. The foundation also gives scholarships to kids that qualify. They must have a certain GPA. Big Money definitely has it going on and he is definitely giving back to the community.

His boy Black is still hanging in there with him. He's the executive director of the organization, and I must admit, he's done a damn good job.

Unlike Money, Black has found him a woman. He's not married yet, but he's shackin' with an older lady. From what I can see, he's happy. Of course, he made it known to his woman that his job and Big Money come first. He tells her that if it wasn't for Money he doesn't know where he'd be. When they visited last month, she even told me that he said he'd die for him. Now that's some deep stuff right there.

It's funny seeing both of them in suits when they come to Atlanta to visit me. At first, Michael was a little jealous of my relationship with Big Money, but he soon realized that Big Money was all the family I had before I met Toi, Amber, and him. He recognized how Big Money had been there for me when no one else was. He really tries to understand the bond that we have. This makes me relieved and happy because I don't know what I'd have done if I had to choose.

Between Big Money and Toi, I don't have to buy much for the baby. They spoil her to the point where Michael and I have to really try to figure out what she doesn't have so we can buy it.

Amber's still married to her man. I don't know how happy they are because they keep drama going. They were the perfect couple in the beginning of their marriage. Once she got to know him she found out he was not loyal to the marriage. He is always screwing or involved with somebody's wife at the health club. Let's just say that he has earned the reputation of the club's "Mandingo." She got so tired of the drama that she was contemplating moving to Atlanta. She eventually decided against it. Her husband said that it was cool for her to move, but he's staying in Florida. He said that they could see each other every other weekend and on holidays. Now, ain't that a bitch?

I'll continue to enjoy my family and stay hopeful of Toi's return. Life ain't fair and it never will be, so just get used to it.

Carolyn Sanders is a registered stockbroker, financial planner, licensed real estate consultant, and insurance agent. She holds an MBA from Texas Southern University and her BS in psychology from Florida A&M University. She is single and resides in Dallas, Texas, with her two children. She is currently working on her second novel, *The Games We Play,* a sequel to *Sins & Secrets.*